The Shifting Sands

D0071492

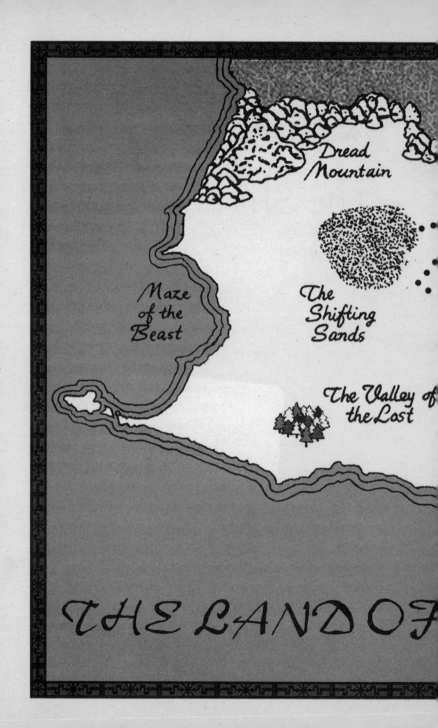

The Shadowlands

The Lake
of Tears

City
of the
Rats

The Forests
of Silence

Del

DELTORA

N
W · E
S

VENTURE INTO DELTORA

The Shifting Sands

EMILY RODDA

Scholastic Inc.

New York Toronto London Auckland Sydney
Mexico City New Delhi Hong Kong Buenos Aires

No part of this publication may be reproduced in whole or in part, or stored in a retrieval system, or transmitted in any form or by any means, electronic, mechanical, photocopying, recording, or otherwise,without written permission of the publisher. For information regarding permission, write to Scholastic Australia, PO Box 579, Lindfield, New South Wales, Australia 2070.

ISBN 0-439-25326-8

Text and graphics copyright © 2000 by Emily Rodda.
Graphics by Kate Rowe.
Cover illustrations copyright © 2000 by Scholastic Australia.
Cover illustrations by Marc McBride.
All rights reserved.

Published by Scholastic Inc., 557 Broadway, New York, NY 10012,
by arrangement with Scholastic Press, an imprint of Scholastic Australia.
SCHOLASTIC and associated logos are trademarks and/or
registered trademarks of Scholastic Inc.

12 11 10   4 5 6 7/0

Printed in the U.S.A.   40

First American edition, July 2001

Contents

The story so far . . .

Sixteen-year-old Lief, fulfilling a pledge made by his father before he was born, is on a great quest to find the seven gems of the magic Belt of Deltora. The gems—an amethyst, a topaz, a diamond, a ruby, an opal, a lapis lazuli, and an emerald—were stolen to open the way for the evil Shadow Lord to invade Deltora. Hidden in fearsome places throughout the land, they must be restored to the Belt before the heir to the throne can be found and the Shadow Lord's tyranny ended.

Lief's companions are the man Barda, who was once a Palace guard, and Jasmine, a wild, orphaned girl of Lief's own age who they met in the fearful Forests of Silence.

So far they have found three gems. The golden topaz, symbol of faith, has the power to contact the spirit world, and to clear the mind. The ruby, symbol of happiness, pales when danger threatens, repels evil spirits, and is an antidote to venom. The opal, gem of hope, gives glimpses of the future.

On their travels, the companions have discovered a secret resistance movement made up of people pledged to defy the Shadow Lord. But servants of the Enemy are everywhere. Some, like his brutal Grey Guards, are easily recognized. Others keep their dark loyalty well hidden.

The three companions are lucky to have escaped the City of the Rats alive. But now they are stranded on the barren plain that surrounds it, having lost all their supplies. The opal has given Lief a terrible vision of their next goal: The Shifting Sands.

Now read on . . .

1 - Flight

It seemed to Lief that they had been walking beside the river forever. Yet only one night and part of a day had passed since he, Barda, and Jasmine had left the City of the Rats in flames. The faint smell of smoke hung in the still air, though the city was now just a blur on the horizon at their backs.

They had long ago discarded the heavy red garments and boots which had saved them from the rats. Walking was easier now. But hunger and exhaustion were making the journey seem endless, and the fact that the landscape never changed did not help. Hour by hour the companions had trudged over bare, baked earth hemmed in on both sides by the waters of Broad River — waters so wide that they could barely see the far banks.

Though all of them badly needed rest, they knew that they had to keep moving. The plume of smoke staining the blue sky at their backs was like a signal to their enemies. It was a sign that something of great importance had happened in the terrible place where the third stone of the Belt of Deltora had been hidden. Should the Shadow Lord become aware that the stone had been taken, his servants would begin searching for the thieves.

And how easily they would find them on this bare plain.

Barda plodded beside Lief, his head lowered. Jasmine walked a little ahead. Now and then she murmured to Filli, who was nestled on her shoulder, but her eyes were fixed on the horizon. She was watching for Kree, the raven. Kree had flown off as dawn broke to survey the land ahead and to look for food.

He had been away for many hours. This boded ill for them. It meant that food and shelter were far distant. But there was nothing to do but keep moving. There was no direction to take but the one they were taking, for the Plain of the Rats lay in a bend of the river, and was bounded on three sides by deep water.

For centuries the rats have been trapped by the river that curves around their plain, thought Lief grimly. And now we are trapped also.

Suddenly Jasmine gave a high, piercing cry. A faint, harsh sound came back in answer.

Lief looked up, and saw a black speck coming towards them through the distant blue. With every

2

moment the speck grew larger, and at last Kree was soaring down, squawking harshly.

He landed on Jasmine's arm and squawked again. Jasmine listened, expressionless. Finally she turned to Lief and Barda.

"Kree says that the plain ends in a broad band of water that is almost as wide as the river itself," she said.

"What?" Appalled, Lief slumped to the ground.

"The plain is an island?" growled Barda. "But it cannot be!" He sat down beside Lief, with a heavy sigh.

Kree ruffled his feathers, and made an annoyed, clucking sound.

"Kree has seen it with his own eyes," snapped Jasmine. "A bar of water joins the two arms of the river. It is very broad, he says, but perhaps not too deep for us to wade. It seemed paler in color than the river, and he could see schools of fish not far from the surface."

"Fish!" Lief's mouth watered at the thought of hot food.

"How far?" he heard Barda ask.

Jasmine shrugged. "Kree thinks that we could reach it by tomorrow, if we move on through the night."

"Then so we will," Barda said grimly, hauling himself to his feet. "At least we cannot easily be seen in the dark. And we have no food, after all. We have no shelter, or anything to sleep upon but the bare earth. So what comfort is there in stopping? We might as well walk till we drop."

✳

So it was that in the pale dawn of the following day they found themselves at the end of the plain, staring, with eyes that prickled with weariness, at a gleaming sheet of water that blocked their path.

"Surely this is not a natural channel," Lief said. "The banks are too straight and even."

"It was dug by human hands," Barda agreed. "Long ago, I would guess, as a barrier against the rats."

Kree soared above them, squawking excitedly.

"On the other side there are trees," murmured Jasmine. "Trees and other growing things."

Without hesitation she stepped into the water, her eyes fixed eagerly on the ragged line of green ahead.

"Jasmine, take care!" Lief called after her. But Jasmine waded on without pausing or turning. The water rose to her waist, then to her chest, but no further. She began moving steadily towards the opposite shore.

Barda and Lief hastened after her, splashing into the cool stream. "When it was my task to keep you out of trouble on the streets of Del, Lief, I thought that you

4

were the most impulsive, troublesome young pest in creation," muttered Barda. "I apologize. Jasmine is just as bad — or worse!"

Lief grinned, then jumped and yelled as something brushed softly against his ankle. He looked down into the water and saw a flurry of sudden movement as several large fish darted away into the shadows.

"They will not hurt you," called Jasmine, without turning around.

"How do you know?" Lief called back. "They could be feeling as hungry as I am. They — "

He broke off as Kree cried out and plummeted towards them, skimming the surface of the water and then soaring up into the air again.

Jasmine stopped, alert, then swung around to face Lief and Barda. "Something is coming from the sky!" she called. "Kree — "

Screeching, the black bird dived towards them once more. Plainly he was terrified.

"What is it?" Frantically, Lief scanned the sky, but could see nothing.

"Something huge! Something very bad!" Jasmine snatched Filli from her shoulder and held him up into the air, a tiny bundle of grey fur, chattering with fear. "Kree!" she shrieked, "Take Filli! Hide him, and yourself!"

And at that moment Lief's straining eyes caught

sight of a black spot on the horizon. It was growing larger by the moment. In seconds Lief could make out a long neck and huge, beating wings.

"Ak-Baba!" hissed Barda. "It has seen the smoke."

Lief's blood seemed to chill in his veins. His father had told him of the Ak-Baba — giant, vulture-like birds that lived a thousand years. Seven of them were the servants of the Shadow Lord. It was they who had carried the gems from the Belt of Deltora to their perilous hiding places.

Obeying Jasmine's command, Kree had snatched up Filli in his claws and was speeding with him to the other side of the band of water. There they could both conceal themselves in the long grass or shelter in a tree.

But Lief, Barda, and Jasmine had nowhere to hide. Behind them was the bare earth of the plain. Before them was a huge sweep of water, glittering in the dawn.

They floundered forward a few steps, but all of them knew it was no use. The Ak-Baba was flying with incredible speed. It would be upon them long before they could reach safety.

Already it could see the smoke of the burning city. When it saw three ragged strangers escaping from the plain it would know at once that they were enemies of the Shadow Lord.

Would it attack them? Or would it simply plunge down, snatch them up in its huge talons, and carry them away to its master? Either way, they were doomed.

The only possible hiding place was under the water. And yet Lief knew that this was no hiding place at all. From the air, the Ak-Baba would be able to see them as clearly as Kree had seen the schools of fish.

"It has not seen us yet," Barda said rapidly. "Its eyes are fixed on the smoke from the city. Lief — your cloak!"

Of course! With wet, clumsy fingers Lief pulled at the strings that fastened his cloak around his throat. At last the cloak floated free.

"Down!" Barda hissed.

All of them took a deep breath and sank below the surface of the stream, holding the cloak over them like a canopy. It drifted above their heads, almost invisible in the water.

They had done their best. But was their best good enough to hide them from the sharp eyes of the Ak-Baba? If it had been dusk, perhaps. But surely, in this bright dawn light, the beast could not fail to notice that one patch of water looked a little different from the rest. Suspicious, it would circle above the place, watching, waiting . . .

And for how long could Lief, Barda, and Jasmine

hold their breath? Sooner or later they would have to rise, gasping, to the surface. Then the monster would strike.

Lief's fingers felt for the clasp of the Belt he wore under his shirt. The Belt of Deltora must not be captured with him. If necessary, he would unloose it and let it fall into the mud at the bottom of the stream. It would be better for it to lie there than for it to fall into the hands of the Shadow Lord again.

Already his lungs felt tight. Already his body was telling him to rise to the surface and breathe. Something nudged at his shoulder and he opened his eyes. Fish were moving all around him — big silver fish, their glassy eyes staring. Their fins and tails buffeted his head and face. They were closing in on him, crowding him.

Then, suddenly, it grew dark. A huge shadow was blocking out the sun.

The Ak-Baba was overhead.

2 ~ Forbidden Fruit

Lief fought down the panic that threatened to engulf him. The shadow of the Ak-Baba had turned the water black. He could no longer see the fish, but he could feel their weight. Dozens were now swimming above the cloak, cutting the companions off from the surface, pressing them down, down . . .

Lief's head was spinning. He began to struggle, his chest aching with the need to breathe. Desperately he pushed at the cloak above his head, but the fish were clustered together so tightly on top of it that they were like a living, moving ceiling, impossible to break.

His struggles became more and more feeble. He could feel himself losing consciousness, his mind drifting away from his body.

Is this, then, how it ends? he thought. After all

we have faced . . . A picture of his mother and father at home flashed through his mind. They would be breakfasting now, in the forge kitchen. Talking of him, perhaps, and of Barda.

They will never know what became of us, Lief thought. Our bones will lie in this mud forever, and with them the Belt of Deltora.

Dimly he became aware of urgent nudges on his legs and chest. The fish were bumping against him. They seemed to be trying to push him upwards. And — the fish above his head were moving aside.

With the last of his strength he forced his trembling legs to straighten. His head broke the surface and he took huge, grateful gulps of air.

At first he could see nothing. The cloak was still draped over his head, clinging to his face. Then it fell away and he was left blinking at Barda and Jasmine, who were as gasping and bedraggled as he.

In terror he looked up. But the Ak-Baba was well past the channel, flying steadily over the plain towards the plume of smoke on the horizon.

"It did not see us!" he croaked, coughing. "It passed us by." He could not believe it.

"Of course," Jasmine grinned, gathering the drifting cloak into a bundle. "When it looked down at the water it saw nothing but a school of fish. Fish that it had seen a hundred times before."

She patted her hands on the rippling surface.

"Ah, you were clever, fish," she laughed. "You hid us well."

The fish swam about her, lazily blowing bubbles. They seemed pleased with themselves.

"I thought they were trying to drown us," said Barda. "And all the time they were disguising us from the Ak-Baba. Whoever heard of fish coming to anyone's aid?"

"These are no ordinary fish," Jasmine assured him. "They are old and wise. They had no love for the rats who turned the plain on one side of their river into a wasteland. And they have no love for the Shadow Lord or his servants, either."

"They *told* you this?" asked Lief, amazed.

The girl shrugged. "They are no ordinary fish," she repeated. "They would speak to you, too, if only you would listen."

Lief stared at the shapes beneath the water and concentrated with all his strength. But all he could hear was rippling and the sound of bubbles.

"I should have known we would not die in the river," he murmured. "On the plain the opal showed me a vision of myself standing in the Shifting Sands. If I am to die anywhere, it will be there."

He felt Barda and Jasmine's eyes upon him. "Does the opal tell what *will* be? Or only what *might* be?" asked Barda abruptly.

Lief shrugged. He did not know.

Kree called from the other side of the channel.

"We must move on," Jasmine said. "The Ak-Baba may return this way."

With the fish swimming ahead of them to make their way easy, the companions waded on across the channel. When at last they had reached the opposite shore they turned and bowed their thanks.

"We owe our lives to you, fish," Jasmine called softly, as Kree flew down to perch on her arm. "We thank you for your kindness."

The fish ducked their own heads, then slowly swam away, their tails waving as if in farewell.

Kree squawked and took flight once more. Lief, Barda, and Jasmine followed him as he fluttered towards a tree that grew beside the water, its long, feathery green branches bending and sweeping the ground.

They pushed through the greenery and found themselves in a small clear space surrounded on all sides by drooping branches. It was like a little green room with the tree's gnarled trunk in its center. Filli sat there waiting for them. He scuttled over to Jasmine and leaped onto her shoulder, chattering with pleasure.

Groaning with relief, the three companions sank to the ground. A thick layer of soft brown leaves cushioned their aching bones. Above them was a roof of green. Around them were walls that whispered in the gentle breeze.

"Safe," murmured Jasmine. But for once there was no need for her to explain what the tree had said. They all felt its peace.

In moments, they were asleep.

※

When Lief woke, he was alone. Birds were calling above his head. It was cool, and the light was dim.

The sun is going down, he thought, shivering. I have slept the whole day through.

Where were Barda and Jasmine, Kree and Filli? Lief crawled over to the hanging branches that curtained his shelter, parted them cautiously and peered out. With a shock he realized that the sun was not setting, but rising. He had slept not just through the day, but through the following night as well!

Jasmine and Barda were coming towards the tree. He guessed they had been searching for food and hoped they had found something. His stomach felt hollow. It seemed a very long time since he had eaten. He pushed through the leaves and ran to meet them.

"Apples!" Barda called, as he approached. "Rather wizened, but sweet enough, and strangely filling."

He threw an apple to Lief, who sank his teeth into it ravenously and soon finished it, core and all.

"It is said that stolen fruit tastes the sweetest," Barda laughed, tossing him another.

"Stolen?" asked Lief, with his mouth full.

"Those trees over there are an orchard," said Barda, pointing behind him. "Jasmine helped herself without troubling to find the owner and ask permission."

Jasmine tossed her head. "The trees are groaning with fruit," she snapped. "They are anxious to be picked. And you can see how withered the apples are. Who could object to us helping ourselves?"

"I am not complaining," said Lief cheerfully. "The last time I had an apple — " He broke off, the sweet fruit suddenly dry in his mouth. The last time he ate an apple he was in Del, feasting with his friends. It had been his sixteenth birthday. It was the day he had said goodbye to childhood, the life he had known, his home, and the parents he loved. How long ago it seemed now.

Jasmine was looking at him curiously. He realized that his expression had grown sad and quickly he turned away. Jasmine had lived alone in the Forests of Silence, with only Filli and Kree for company. She had seen her parents taken away by Grey Guards, and braved terrors without number from her earliest childhood. He was sure that his homesickness would seem a weak and childish thing to her.

He took another bite of his apple, then jumped as a high-pitched voice rang out.

"Thieves!"

Lief squinted against the shimmering dawn light. Something was rolling through the long grass towards them, shrieking. As it drew closer he realized that it was a little old woman. She was so plump, and

14

so wrapped and bundled in shawls, that she seemed completely round. Thin brown hair was screwed up into a tiny topknot on her head. Her face was creased and crinkled all over like a wizened apple, and red with anger. She was frowning furiously, shaking her fist.

"Thieves!" she shrieked. "Vagabonds! Give them back! Give them back!"

The three companions stared at her, open-mouthed.

"You stole my apples!" the old women shrieked. "You stole my beauties while my guards slept. Where are they? Give them to me!"

Silently, Jasmine passed over the three apples that remained in her hands. The woman clasped them to her chest and glared.

"Cheat! Where are the others?" she shouted. "Where are the other six? Every apple is numbered. Every one must be accounted for. How else can I fill my quota? Nine fruit you took, and nine must be returned."

Barda cleared his throat. "I am very sorry, madam, but we cannot return them. I fear they are already eaten."

"*Eaten??*"

The old woman seemed to swell, and went so red that Lief feared she might explode.

"We — we beg your pardon," he stammered. "We were so hungry, and — "

The old woman threw back her head, raised her arms, shook her shawls, and gave a terrible, high-pitched cry.

Immediately she was surrounded by a dark, whirling, humming cloud.

Bees. Thousands of bees. They had been riding on her back, clustered under her shawls. Now they were swarming in the air around her, waiting for the order to attack.

3 - The Road to Rithmere

Lief, Barda, and Jasmine stumbled back. The cloud of bees surged this way and that, making patterns in the air behind the old woman's head. Their buzzing was like the threatening growl of a great animal.

"You thought I was unprotected, did you?" screeched the old woman. "You thought you could steal from me without fear. My guards are small, but many, and act with one mind. You will suffer death by a thousand stings for what you have done."

Jasmine was desperately feeling in her pockets. She found what she was looking for and held out her hand. Gold and silver coins gleamed in the sunlight.

"Will you take these for your apples?" she asked.

The old woman gave a start. Her eyes narrowed. "If you have money, why do you steal?" she de-

17

manded. But her wrinkled hand shot out and took the coins.

"No!" Lief exclaimed, lunging forward without thinking. "That money is all we have. You cannot take it all for a few dried-up apples!"

The bees surged at him, buzzing dangerously.

"Softly, boy, softly. Gently, gently!" cackled the old woman. "My guards do not like sudden movements, and are easily angered. Why, even I must use smoke to calm them when I take their honey from the hive. Even I."

She made a soft sound and the cloud of bees behind her shrank and disappeared as the creatures returned to the folds of her shawls. She tucked the coins carefully away and scowled at the companions.

"Let this be a lesson to you!" she ordered. "And tell all your fellow vagabonds that the next thieves who come here will receive no mercy."

Lief, Barda, and Jasmine hesitated.

She shook her fist at them. "Go on!" she shrilled. "Get back to the road where you came from."

"We did not come from the road, old woman! And we are not thieves, either!" Jasmine cried.

The woman grew very still. "If you did not come from the road, then where did you come from?" she murmured after a moment. "There is no other way to my orchard. Except . . ."

Suddenly she reached out and grasped the edge of Lief's cloak. Feeling its dampness, she gasped and slowly raised her head to look across the water and away to the horizon where a faint drift of smoke still rose over the Plain of the Rats.

A look of dread crossed her wrinkled face.

"Who are you?" she whispered. Then she held up her hand. "No — do not tell me. Just go! If you are seen here not even my bees will be able to protect me."

"How do we find the road?" asked Lief quickly.

She pointed to the orchard behind her. "Go through the orchard. There is a gate on the far side. Hurry! And forget what I said. Tell no one you were here."

"You can count on that," said Barda. "As I presume we can count on you forgetting you ever saw us?"

She nodded silently. The three companions turned and strode away across the grass. As they reached the trees they heard a shout and looked back. The strange old woman was standing, round as a ball, in a cloud of bees, staring after them.

"Good fortune!" she cried, raising her arm.

They lifted their own arms in reply, and went on.

"It is all very well to wish us good fortune now," complained Jasmine as they threaded their way through the apple trees. "A few moments ago she was threatening to have us stung to death by her bees. And she did not offer to return our money."

Barda shrugged. "Who knows what troubles she has suffered? Perhaps she is right to be suspicious of strangers. Except for the bees she seems all alone here."

"She spoke of a 'quota' that had to be filled," Lief said slowly, as they reached the end of the orchard and let themselves through a gate that led to a winding, tree-lined track. "It sounds as though she has to grow a certain number of apples."

"Or make something from them," said Barda. He closed the gate behind them and nodded towards a sign fixed to the old wood.

Queen Bee Cider
The Champion's Choice

Made from genuine tree-aged cider apples

NO ENTRY
WITHOUT PERMISSION

"Queen Bee Cider was a drink much prized among the guards and acrobats when I was at the palace in Del," Barda went on. "It gave extra strength to anyone who drank it. It seems that it is made here — by our friend back there, who is no doubt Queen Bee herself."

Lief sighed. "I wish that she had given us a glass or two before sending us on our way."

Indeed, all of them were tired and in low spirits as they trudged along the track, talking in low voices. They knew that their next goal must be the Shifting Sands. But how they were to reach it was a mystery.

In all their minds was the thought that they had no money, no food, no blankets, no packs — nothing but the map Lief's father had drawn for him, their weapons, and the ragged clothes on their backs.

And the Belt of Deltora, Lief reminded himself. But the Belt, for all its power, for all that three stones now glimmered in their places along its length, could not fill their bellies or shelter them from the weather.

"The opal gives glimpses of the future," said Jasmine, after a moment. "Surely it can tell us what is ahead?"

But Lief was unwilling to touch the opal. His vision of the Shifting Sands still haunted him. He had no wish to experience it again.

"We do not need to see into the future to know that we need help," he said, staring straight ahead.

21

"We need supplies and a safe place to rest for a while. Let us think only of that for now."

He expected Jasmine to argue, but when he glanced at her he saw that she had stopped listening to him and was concentrating on something else.

"I hear carts and the sound of feet," she announced finally. "Voices, too. There is a larger road ahead."

Sure enough, in a few more minutes the winding trail met a broad, straight highway. Cautiously they looked both ways along its length. A horse-drawn cart was approaching from the right with several men and women walking beside it.

"It seems there are others going our way," muttered Barda. "They look harmless enough. But still it might be wise to wait until they have passed. We cannot afford too many questions until we are well away from here."

They crouched among the trees and watched while the cart came closer. It was worn and rickety, and the horse that pulled it was old and plodding. But the people — those walking beside it as well as those who jolted along inside — were talking and laughing with one another as though all was well with the world.

Lief heard the name "Rithmere" repeated several times as the cart passed by. It was clear that Rithmere was a town, and that the people were looking forward to reaching it. His spirits rose.

"There must be a festival or fair being held in this Rithmere place," he whispered.

"A festival in these days?" grunted Barda. "I cannot believe it. But still, if Rithmere is to the left along this road, it is on our way to the Shifting Sands. And a town is what we need — the larger the better."

"Why?" hissed Jasmine, who far preferred the open countryside.

"In a town we can lose ourselves in the crowd and earn money for new supplies. Or beg for it."

"*Beg?*" exclaimed Lief, horrified.

Barda glanced at him, a grim smile tweaking the corner of his mouth. "There are times when pride must be put aside in a good cause," he said.

Lief mumbled an apology. How could he have forgotten that Barda had spent years disguised as a beggar in Del?

When the cart was well past, the companions crept out from the trees and began to follow it. They had not gone far before Lief saw something lying on the ground.

It was a notice. Curious, he picked it up:

THE RITHMERE GAMES

Come one, come all!
Test your strength and skill!

*100 GOLD COINS
TO EVERY FINALIST!

*1000 GOLD COINS
TO GRAND WINNER!!!

Lief showed the notice to Barda and Jasmine. His heart was thudding with excitement.

"Here is our answer!" he said. "Here is our chance to earn the money we need, and more. We will enter the Games. And we will win!"

4 - Lost in the Crowd

Days later, when Rithmere was at last in sight, Lief was not feeling so hopeful. The way had been long and weary, and he was very hungry. Berries growing at the side of the road were the only food the companions had been able to find, and they were few. Travellers who had passed along the highway before them had almost stripped the bushes bare.

The longer they had walked, the more crowded the highway had become. Many other people were moving towards Rithmere. Some were as ill-prepared for the journey as Lief, Barda, and Jasmine. Their clothes were tattered and they had little or nothing to eat. A few, famished and exhausted, fell by the roadside in despair.

The companions managed to keep moving, stopping often for rests. They spoke to their fellow travellers as little as possible. Though they were feeling safer concealed in a crowd, they still felt it wise to avoid questions about where they had come from.

They kept their ears open, however, and quickly learned that the Games had been held every year for the past ten years. Their fame had grown and spread — now hopeful contestants came from everywhere to seek their fortune at Rithmere. The friends also learned, to their relief, that Grey Guards were seldom seen in the town while the Games were in progress.

"They know better than to interfere with something the people like so much," Lief heard a tall, red-haired woman say to her companion, a giant of a man whose muscles bulged through his ragged shirt as he bent to tighten the laces of his boot.

The man nodded. "A thousand gold coins," he muttered. "Or even a hundred! Think of the difference it would make to us — and to all at home." He finished tying his lace, straightened, and gritted his teeth as he stared at the city ahead. "This year we will be finalists at least, Joanna. I feel it."

"You have never been stronger, Orwen," the woman agreed affectionately. "And I, too, have a good chance. Last year I was not watchful enough. I let that vixen Brianne of Lees trip me. It will not happen again."

Orwen put his great arm around her shoulders. "You cannot blame yourself for losing to Brianne. After all, she went on to become Champion. She is a great fighter. And think how hard the people of Lees worked to prepare her."

"She was treated like a queen, they say," said Joanna bitterly. "Extra food, no duties except her training. Her people thought she would be their salvation. And what did she do? Ran off with the money as soon as she had it in her hand. Can you believe it?"

"Of course," the man said grimly. "A thousand gold pieces is a great fortune, Joanna. Very few Games Champions return to their old homes after their win. Most do not want to share their wealth, so they hurry away with it to start a new life elsewhere."

"But you would never do that, Orwen," Joanna protested fiercely. "And neither would I. I would *never* leave my people in poverty while I could help them. I would rather throw myself into the Shifting Sands."

Lief stiffened at her last words and glanced at Jasmine and Barda to see if they had heard.

Joanna and Orwen strode on, shoulder to shoulder, towering above the rest of the crowd.

"That she mentions the Shifting Sands means nothing, Lief," Barda said in a low voice, looking after them. "The Sands are as familiar a nightmare to folk who live in these parts as the Forests of Silence are to the people of Del."

His face was grim, deeply marked with lines of weariness. "A more important matter is to decide whether we are wasting our time trying to compete with such as Joanna and Orwen. In our present state — "

"We have to try," Lief mumbled, though his own heart was very heavy.

"There is no point in talking of this now!" Jasmine broke in impatiently. "Whether we compete in the Games or not, we must enter the city. We must get some food — even if we have to steal it. What else are we to do?"

✳

Rithmere seethed with people. Stalls lined the narrow streets, packed together, filling every available space, their owners shouting of what they had to sell and watching their goods with eagle-sharp eyes.

The noise was deafening. Musicians, dancers, fire-eaters, and jugglers performed on every corner, their hats set out in front of them to catch coins thrown by passersby. Some had animals — snakes, dogs, even dancing bears, as well as strange creatures the companions had never seen before — to help them attract attention.

The noise, the smells, the bright colors, the confusion, made Lief, already light-headed with hunger, feel faint and sick. Faces in the crowd seemed to loom out at him as he stumbled along. Some he recognized from the highway. Most were strange to him.

Everywhere were the hunched forms of beggars, their gaunt faces turned up pleadingly, their hands outstretched. Some were blind, or had missing limbs. Others were simply starving. Most people paid no attention to them at all, stepping over them as if they were piles of rubbish.

"Hey, girl! You with the black bird! Over here!"

The hoarse shout had come from somewhere very near. They looked around, startled.

A fat man with long, greasy hair was beckoning urgently to Jasmine. The three companions edged through the crowd towards him, wondering what he wanted. As they drew closer they saw that he was sitting at a small table which had been covered by a red cloth that reached the ground. Leaning against the wall behind him was a pair of crutches. On the table stood a perch, a basket of painted wooden birds, and a wheel decorated with brightly colored pictures of birds and coins.

It was plainly some sort of gambling game.

"Like to make some money, little lovely?" the man shouted above the noise of the crowd.

Jasmine frowned and said nothing.

"She cannot play," Lief shouted back. "Unless it costs nothing."

The man snorted. "How would I make my living that way, young fellow-me-lad? No, no. One silver coin for a spin of the wheel, that is my price. But I am not asking your friend to play. No one can play at present. My bird just died on me. See?" He held up a dead pigeon by its feet and swung it in front of their noses.

Jasmine glared at him, stony-faced. The man's mouth turned down mournfully. "Sad, isn't it?" he said. "Sad for Beakie-Boy, sadder for me. I need a bird to turn the wheel. That's the game. Beat the Bird, you see? I have another two pigeons back in my lodgings, but if I go and fetch one now I'll lose my spot. Lose half a day's earnings. Can't afford that, can I?"

His small eyes narrowed as he looked Jasmine up and down. "You and your friends look as if you could do with a good meal inside you," he said slyly. "Well, I will help you out."

He threw the dead pigeon on the ground, kicked it under the table, and pointed at Kree. "I will buy your bird. How much do you want for him?"

5 - Win and Lose

Jasmine shook her head. "Kree is not for sale," she said firmly, and turned to go. The fat man clutched at the sleeve of her jacket.

"Don't turn your back on me, little lovely," he whined. "Don't turn your back on poor old Ferdinand, for pity's sake."

Kree put his head to one side and looked at the man carefully. Then he hopped onto the table and stalked right up to him, inspecting him closely, his head darting this way and that. After a moment he squawked loudly.

Jasmine glanced at Lief and Barda, then back at Ferdinand. "Kree says, how much would you give for his help just for today?" she said.

The fat man laughed. "Talks to you, does he?" he jeered disbelievingly. "Well now, that is something you don't see every day."

He took a small tin from his pocket, opened it, and took out a silver coin. "Tell him from me that I'll give him this if he turns the wheel till sunset. Would that suit him?"

Kree flew back to perch on Jasmine's arm and squawked again. Jasmine nodded slowly. "For one silver coin, Kree will turn the wheel thirty times. If you want him to do more, you pay again."

"That is robbery!" Ferdinand exclaimed.

"It is his price," said Jasmine calmly.

Ferdinand's face crumpled, and he buried it in his hands. "Ah, you are a cruel girl! Cruel to a poor unfortunate trying to make a living," he mumbled. "My last hope is gone. I will starve, and my birds with me." His shoulders shook as he began to sob.

Jasmine shrugged, apparently quite unmoved. Lief, glancing at Ferdinand's crutches propped against the wall, felt very uncomfortable.

"It seems harsh, Jasmine," he whispered in her ear. "Could you not — ?"

"He is acting. He can afford ten times as much," Jasmine hissed back. "Kree says he has a purse at his belt that is bulging with coins. It is hidden from us by the cloth that covers the table. Just wait."

Sure enough, when after a moment the fat man peeped through his fingers and saw that Jasmine was not going to change her mind, he stopped pretending to sob and took his hands away from his face. "Very well," he snapped, in quite a different voice. "For a bird, he drives a hard bargain. Put him on the perch."

"The money first, if you please," Barda put in quickly.

Ferdinand shot him an angry look, then, with much groaning and sighing, passed the silver coin he had taken from the tin to Jasmine.

Satisfied, Kree fluttered onto the perch.

"Stand aside, you three," Ferdinand said sharply. "Make way for the customers."

The companions did as they were told, but remained close by so that they could watch what happened. None of them trusted Ferdinand. The smell of food wafting from a nearby stall made Lief's mouth water, but he knew that they could not buy anything with the silver coin until Kree was safely back on Jasmine's arm.

"Roll up, roll up!" Ferdinand bellowed. "Beat the bird and win! One silver coin for a spin of the wheel! Every player wins a prize!"

A small crowd began to cluster around his table as he began pointing at the numbers on the coins painted around the wheel. "Two silver pieces for one!" he shouted. "Or would you prefer three silver pieces? Or four? Yes, ladies and gentlemen, boys and girls. Four silver pieces for one!"

People began feeling in their pockets for coins.

Ferdinand's pudgy hand moved around the

wheel, his finger stabbing at one number after another. "But why stop at four?" he shouted. "This is your lucky day! Why, you could win five, six, or *ten* silver pieces!" He tore at his hair and rolled his eyes. His voice rose to a shriek. "Ten silver coins for one! A prize for every player! Why do I do it? I must be losing my wits!"

Several people pressed forward, holding out their money. Lief moved restlessly.

"Perhaps we should use our coin on the game," he muttered to Barda. "We could double our money. Or even better!"

Barda smiled at him pityingly. "Or, which is more likely, we could lose our coin and finish with nothing but a worthless wooden bird," he said. "If the wheel stops at a bird instead of a coin . . ."

Lief was not convinced. Especially when he saw Kree spin the wheel for the first time, hitting it sharply with his beak. The wheel spun smoothly around and around. The player, an eager-looking woman with flowing hair, watched anxiously, then cried out with delight as the wheel stopped and the marker showed that she had won two coins.

"She has beaten the bird!" shrieked Ferdinand, scrabbling in his money tin and handing the woman her prize. "Oh, mercy me!" He turned to Kree and shook his fist. "Try harder!" he scolded. "You will ruin me!"

The crowd laughed. Another player stepped forward. Kree spun the wheel again. The second player was even luckier than the first, winning three coins.

"This bird is hopeless!" Ferdinand howled in despair. "Oh, what will I do?"

After that, he could not take his customers' money fast enough. People crowded in front of his table, eager for their turn to play.

Kree spun the wheel again and again. And, somehow, no one else seemed to have the luck of the first two players. More and more often the wheel would stop at a bird picture, and the disappointed player would creep away clutching a wooden bird. Only rarely did the marker point to a picture of a coin, and when it did it was usually a coin marked "1" or "2."

But whenever that happened Ferdinand would make an enormous fuss, congratulating the winner, saying he was ruined, shouting at Kree for playing badly, and fretting that next time the prize would be even bigger.

But the pile of silver in the money tin was growing. Every few minutes, Ferdinand would quietly take some coins and tuck them away in the purse at his belt. And still the players pressed forward, eager to try their luck.

"No wonder his purse is bulging," Jasmine muttered in disgust. "Why do these people give him their money? Some of them are plainly very poor. Can they not see that he wins far more often than they do?"

"Ferdinand only makes noise when players win," said Barda heavily. "The losers are ignored and quickly forgotten."

Jasmine made a disgusted face. "Kree has made twenty-nine turns," she said. "After one more, we can take him back. I have no wish to go on with this. I do not like Ferdinand, or his wheel. Do you agree?"

Barda nodded, and Lief did also. However much they needed money, neither of them wanted to help Ferdinand any longer.

Barda pointed to a banner fixed high to a building a little way along the road.

OFFICIAL GAMES INN
*Bed and Board *Competitors Only
*Amazing Prices!

"We may find shelter and some food there," he suggested. "They may let us work for our keep. At least we can try."

Kree had spun the wheel for a final time. The player, a thin-faced man with deep shadows under his eyes, watched desperately as it slowed. When it stopped at the picture of a bird, and Ferdinand handed him the little wooden trinket, his mouth quivered and he slunk away, his bony shoulders bowed.

Jasmine stepped to the table and held out her arm for Kree. "The thirty turns have been made, Ferdinand," she said. "We must go now."

But Ferdinand, his plump face glistening with sweat and greed, turned his small eyes towards her and shook his head violently.

"You cannot go," he spat. "I need the bird. He is the best I have ever had. Look at the crowd! You cannot take him!"

His arm shot out, his pudgy hand grasping at Kree's feet. But Kree fluttered from his perch just in time, landing at the edge of the table.

"Come back here!" hissed Ferdinand, reaching for him. Kree bent his head and with his sharp beak tweaked at the red cloth that covered the table. As it was pulled aside, the crowd gasped, then began to roar with anger.

For on the ground under the table was a pedal with some wires that led up through the tabletop to the wheel.

"He can stop and start the wheel as he wills!" someone shouted. "He uses his feet. See? He cheats!"

The crowd pressed forward angrily. Kree hopped hastily onto Jasmine's arm. Ferdinand swept up the wheel and leaped to his feet, tipping over the table.

The wooden birds and the tin of silver coins crashed to the ground as he took to his heels, hurtling down the street with surprising speed, the wheel tucked under his arm, the remains of its cheating wires trailing. Some of his customers stopped to pick up the money which was rolling everywhere. Most sped off in pursuit of the escaping man, shouting in fury.

6 - Berry, Birdie, and Twig

Lief looked after them, open-mouthed. "Why, there is nothing wrong with Ferdinand's legs at all!" he exclaimed. "He has left his crutches behind — and he is running!"

"A cheat in every way," Barda snorted. "I hope his customers catch him. We are fortunate that they did not blame Kree and turn on us."

"Fortunate, too, that you made Ferdinand pay us in advance," murmured Jasmine. She was scanning the roadway, searching for coins. But the crowd had picked the ground clean and all she found was one wooden bird. She picked it up and tucked it away in her pocket with her other treasures. For Jasmine, nothing was too small to be of use.

Guided by the banner billowing high above the heads of the crowd, they made their way to the Champion Inn. They entered the door and to their surprise found themselves in a very small closed room. A plump woman in a bright green dress decorated with many frills and ribbons rose from behind a desk in one corner and bustled towards them, the large bunch of keys at her waist jingling importantly.

"Good-day!" she cried, in a friendly way. "I am Mother Brightly, your hostess. Please forgive me, but before I can welcome you here I must ask if you are competitors in the Games."

"We wish to be," said Barda cautiously. "But we are strangers in these parts, and do not know how to enter."

"Why, then, you have come to the right place!" Mother Brightly beamed. "This is the official Games inn. Here you can register as competitors, and stay until the Games begin tomorrow."

The companions exchanged glances. It sounded wonderful, but . . .

"We have only one silver coin between us," Barda admitted reluctantly. "We were hoping that perhaps we could work for our keep."

The woman flapped her hands at him, shaking her head. "Work? Nonsense!" she exclaimed. "You must rest and eat so that you can do your best in the Games. If one silver coin is all you have, one silver coin is the price you will pay. Competitors pay only what they can afford at the Champion Inn."

Before the companions could say any more she hurried back to the desk, beckoning them to follow.

She sat down, pulled a large open book towards her and took up a pen. "Name and town?" she asked briskly, glancing at Barda.

Lief caught his breath. He, Barda, and Jasmine had decided that it would be unwise to give their real names when they entered the Games. But they had not realized that they would have to think of false names so soon.

Mother Brightly was waiting, pen poised and eyebrows raised.

"Ah . . . my name is — Berry. Of Bushtown," stammered Barda.

The woman wrote, frowning slightly. "I have not heard of Bushtown before," she said.

"It is — to the north," Barda answered. "My friends — Birdie and — and Twig — are also from there."

He glanced nervously at Jasmine and Lief, who were both glaring at him, but Mother Brightly nodded, writing busily and apparently quite satisfied.

"Now," she said, jumping up with the book clutched under her arm. "Follow me, if you please!"

Things were moving very fast. Feeling rather dazed, Lief, Barda, and Jasmine followed her into another room where stood a large set of scales, a long rule, and a big cupboard.

"Please give me your weapons," Mother Brightly said, taking a key from the bunch at her waist and unlocking the cupboard. Then, as the companions hesitated, she clapped her hands sharply and raised her voice. "I must insist! It is forbidden to carry weapons in the Champion Inn."

Unwillingly, Lief and Barda unbuckled their swords, and Jasmine handed over the dagger she wore at her belt. Mother Brightly locked the weapons in the cupboard, nodding approvingly. "Do not fear," she said in a calmer voice. "They will be quite safe here, and returned to you before you leave. Now — your measurements."

She weighed Lief, Barda, and Jasmine in turn, and measured their heights, writing all the details down in her book. She felt their muscles and looked carefully at their hands and feet. Then she nodded, pleased.

"You need food and rest, my dears, but otherwise you are all strong, and should do well," she said. "I thought so, when first I saw you. One last thing. Your special talents. What are they?"

She waited with her head on one side.

Lief, Barda, and Jasmine glanced at one another. They were not quite sure what the woman meant.

"I — can climb," said Jasmine hesitantly at last. "I can balance on high places, swing, jump . . ."

"Excellent, Birdie!" said Mother Brightly, and wrote "AGILITY" beside Jasmine's false name. She turned to Barda. "And you, Berry? Let me guess. Your talent would be strength. Am I right?"

Barda shrugged and nodded. The woman beamed, and wrote again. Then she looked at Lief. "And Twig?" she enquired.

Lief felt his face growing hot and knew that he was blushing. What had possessed Barda to give him such an absurd name? And what was his special talent? He was not sure that he had one.

"Speed," Barda said quickly. "My friend is very fast on his feet, and can jump, duck, and dodge with the best."

"Perfect!" cried Mother Brightly, writing "SPEED" beside the name "Twig of Bushtown." "Agility, strength, and speed. Why, together you three must be a fine team. Now, wait here a moment. I will not be long."

She bustled out of the room again. The companions looked at one another. All of them were bewildered at this sudden change in their fortunes.

"No wonder people flock to Rithmere," said Lief in a low voice. "It is surprising that the whole of Deltora is not here. Why, at the very least folk get free food and a bed for a while."

"So long as they are willing to compete," Barda whispered back. "I have a feeling that these Games may be more difficult, or more dangerous, than we expect."

"No running or jumping race could be more dangerous than what we have been through," hissed

Jasmine. "The most difficult thing about this will be remembering to answer to those stupid names you chose for us, Barda."

"Yes," Lief agreed. "Twig! Could you think of nothing better?"

"I was taken by surprise and said the first things that came into my head," Barda growled. "If I had hesitated she would have known I was lying."

At that moment Mother Brightly came rustling into the room again. With her she brought three colored strips of cloth — a red, a green, and a blue. She tied the red band around Barda's wrist, the green band around Lief's wrist, and the blue around Jasmine's. Their false names had been written on their bands, with their heights and weights underneath.

"Do not take your wristbands off, even to sleep," Mother Brightly advised. "They mark you as official competitors, show your special talent, and entitle you to food, drink, and entrance to the Games. Now — you will want to eat, I do not doubt, and rest after your journey. The silver coin, if you please?"

Jasmine handed her the coin and in return received a key labelled with the number 77. "This is the key to your room," Mother Brightly said. "A lucky number indeed. Keep it safe."

As they nodded she hesitated, nibbling at her bottom lip as if trying to make up her mind about something. Then, suddenly, she glanced behind her to make sure they were alone and leaned towards them with a rustle of green frills.

"Now — I do not say this to every competitor, but you are strangers to the Games, and I have taken a liking to you," she whispered. "Trust no one, however friendly. And keep your door locked at all times — especially at night. We do not want any . . . accidents."

She put a finger to her lips, then turned and hurried off again, beckoning them to follow.

Wondering, they followed her down a hallway to a large dining room, where a great number of people wearing red, blue, and green wristbands were eating and drinking with gusto. Many of the diners looked up and stared, their faces alive with curiosity, challenge, suspicion, or menace. Most of them were very large and looked extremely strong, though there were some smaller, leaner men and women as well.

Lief lifted his chin and looked around proudly, determined to show that he was not nervous or afraid. At a center table he saw Joanna and Orwen, the two tall companions he had seen on the highway. Then he gave a start. Sitting near to them, though alone, was another person he knew.

It was the dark, scarred traveller the companions had seen at Tom's shop, on their way to the City of the Rats. The man's hard eyes were fixed on the newcomers, but he gave no sign that he recognized them.

"Help yourselves to anything you fancy, my

dears," Mother Brightly said, pointing to a long bench at the side of the room where dishes stood keeping warm over low flames. "Eat, then rest. Do all you can to be fit for tomorrow. I have great hopes for you three! To me, you have the look of finalists. And I have seen many come and go."

She had not troubled to lower her voice, and Lief fidgeted as the gazes of the other competitors grew even more alert. They had all heard what she had said.

"Now, I must return to my post," Mother Brightly said. "It grows late, but new competitors could arrive even now. A bell will wake you for breakfast tomorrow. A second bell, an hour later, will call you to the Games."

She turned to go. Suddenly unwilling to be left alone in the unfriendly room, Lief spoke to delay her. "Before you go, Mother Brightly, could you advise us on which events we should try for?" he asked.

The woman's eyebrows rose as she stared at him. "But surely you know? You do not choose for yourselves who you will fight."

"Fight?" Lief echoed faintly.

Mother Brightly nodded. "You fight those chosen for you — others who match your height, weight, and special talent," she said. "At least at first. Of course, if you win your early rounds, you will at last fight competitors of all kinds."

She clasped her hands. Her eyes were sparkling.

"Those events are always the most exciting of all. Agility against strength. Speed against agility. Wits against weight. Large against small. Sometimes the contests last for many hours. Two years ago there was a final that lasted a day and a night — ah, a bloody battle that was. The loser, poor fellow, lost his leg in the end, for it was smashed to pieces. But of course he had his hundred gold coins as comfort. And it was wonderful entertainment, I assure you!"

She nodded to them happily and trotted off. The door clicked shut behind her.

7 ~ Trouble

The companions eyed one another in silence. "So," said Barda at last. "Now we know why the whole of Deltora does not enter the Rithmere Games. Most people have no wish to be pounded into the ground for sport."

Lief glanced at the place where the scar-faced man had been sitting, ready to point him out to Jasmine and Barda, but the chair was pushed back and empty. The man had gone.

"I think we should leave here," he said slowly. "We cannot risk serious injury just to make money. We will have to get supplies another way."

Jasmine shook her head. "I am not leaving until I eat," she announced. "I am very hungry, and so is Filli."

Barda and Lief looked at each other. The idea of food was very tempting. "Mother Brightly has our silver coin," Lief murmured. "It will surely pay for one meal."

So it was decided. They helped themselves to food, heaping their plates high. Then they found a place to sit and began to eat gratefully. The food was very good. Jugs of Queen Bee Cider stood on the table, and they drank mug after mug of its bubbling sweetness.

Concentrating on their meal they spoke little to one another at first, and no one spoke to them. But Lief's neck prickled, and he knew that dozens of pairs of eyes were still trained on him. The other competitors were trying to judge how dangerous an opponent he would be. You do not have to worry, he told them silently. Soon I will be gone.

The dining hall had almost emptied by the time they finished their meal. His hunger satisfied at last, Lief found that he was longing for sleep. Barda and Jasmine were also yawning, but they all knew that they could not stay in the inn. Unwillingly they rose to their feet and went to the door through which they had come, aware that their every step was being watched.

"I will be glad to be out of here, but I do not look forward to telling Mother Brightly that we have changed our minds," Lief murmured uncomfortably.

Jasmine laughed. "Because she will be angry with us? What does it matter?"

Barda pushed at the door, but it did not budge. It seemed to be locked from the outside.

"Not that way," a slow, deep voice said behind them. "The sleeping rooms and training areas are through there." They turned and saw the huge figure of Orwen. He was pointing to another door at the end of the room.

"We do not want the sleeping rooms or the training areas," Jasmine answered abruptly. "We want to leave the inn."

Orwen gazed at her blankly for a moment. Then, finally, he shook his head. "You are competitors," he said. "You cannot leave."

Lief decided that the big man must be slow-witted. "We have changed our minds, Orwen," he said gently. "We no longer wish to compete in the Games. We wish to leave Rithmere and go on our way."

But again Orwen shook his head. "You cannot change your minds," he said. "Your names are in the book. You have your wristbands. You have eaten and drunk in the dining hall. They will not let you leave."

"Do you mean we are *prisoners*?" Barda demanded.

Orwen shrugged his great shoulders. "The rest of us wish to be here," he said. "We do not think of ourselves as prisoners. But certainly we are not free to come and go as we please."

With a nod of farewell, he turned and left them.

Angrily, Jasmine beat on the door with her fists. It shuddered and its frame rattled, but no one came.

"What shall we do now?" demanded Lief.

"We will go quietly to our room," said Barda evenly. "Our minds are working slowly now, because we are tired. We will sleep, and when we wake we will find a way out, never fear."

The room was silent and everyone was staring as they strode to the door at the back of the dining hall and went out. Signs directed them up some stairs to the sleeping quarters floor. Once there, they began to walk through a maze of door-lined hallways, looking for Room 77.

Rugs cushioned their feet and the hallways were well lit and silent, but as they walked, Lief began to feel more and more uncomfortable. Sudden draughts kept striking chill on his legs. The back of his neck was tingling. He was sure that doors were stealthily opening behind him and that unfriendly eyes were peering after him. Several times he spun around to try to catch the spies, but there was never anything to be seen.

"Just keep walking," said Barda loudly. "Let the fools look. What does it matter to us?"

"Someone is following us, also," Jasmine breathed. "I feel it. That woman should not have said what she did about us. I fear that someone has decided to put us out of the way before the Games even begin."

Automatically, Lief's hand moved to his sword, but of course the weapon was missing — locked away in Mother Brightly's cupboard.

The numbers on the doors beside him were 65 and 66. Ahead there was a turn in the hallway. "Our room cannot be far away now," he whispered. "Once we reach it we will be safe."

They quickened their pace. In moments they had reached the turn in the hallway. They hurried around the corner and found themselves in a short, dead-end corridor. Seeing that Room 77 was right at the end, they began moving towards it.

Then the light went out.

Kree screeched a warning. In the blackness, Lief twisted and leaped sideways, flattening himself against the wall. He felt a glancing blow on his shoulder. He heard Barda shout. He heard a thump and a crash and an angry hiss of pain. There was a scrabbling, scuffling noise and the sound of running feet. Then silence.

"Lief! Barda!" It was Jasmine's voice. "Are you — ?"

Lief answered, and to his relief heard Barda mutter also. Then, as suddenly as it had gone out, the light went on again. Shading his eyes against the sudden glare, Lief blinked at Barda who was staggering to his feet, pulling a crumpled paper from his pocket.

Behind him stood Jasmine, her hair wildly tangled. Her left hand was held up protectively to where

Filli hid under her jacket. In her right hand she held her second dagger — the one she usually kept hidden. Its tip was stained with red. She was frowning fiercely, looking back along the hallway. Lief followed her gaze and saw that a trail of red drops marked the floor all the way to the corner.

"Good! I thought I had drawn blood, but I was not certain. That will teach them that we are not easy marks," Jasmine hissed. "Cowards, to attack us from behind, in the dark!"

"They took our key," said Barda grimly. "And they left this in its place." He showed them the paper he was holding.

The companions looked around them. The hallway was silent. None of the doors had opened.

"Well?" Lief asked, after a moment. "What are we to do about this?"

But he already knew the answer. He could feel himself simmering with anger. He could see the fire in Jasmine's eyes, and the stubborn set of Barda's jaw.

"Whoever attacked us made a mistake," Jasmine said, loudly enough for anyone listening to hear. "Whatever we may have thought before, we will certainly now not be running away from this contest."

"And it will not be *we* who will regret it!" Barda added, just as loudly.

They walked slowly to the door marked 77. It opened when Barda turned the knob and they went into the small, neat room beyond.

It was light and bright, with a gaily colored rug on the floor, but the barred window made it look like a prison cell. The only pieces of furniture were three beds with bright red covers and a small, heavy cupboard.

"Whoever has taken our key thinks, perhaps, to make us lie awake all night, fearing attack," muttered Lief.

"Then he is foolish," Barda snapped. "We will sleep well. We will fear nothing." He put his shoulder against the cupboard and pushed it against the door.

With relief they fell on their beds and slept. As Barda had predicted, they slept soundly. If there were any small sounds outside their door in the darkness of the night, they were not disturbed. They slept on, safe in the knowledge that no one could enter the room without waking them.

But, as Barda had said, they were very tired, and were thinking slowly. Focused on the danger of attack, they had forgotten one thing.

Just as a key can unlock a door, so it can lock it. When the wakening bell rang in the morning and they moved the cupboard aside they found the door locked fast.

Their unknown enemy had found another way of seeing that they did not win in the Games. He had decided to prevent them attending the Games at all.

8 - The Games

For a long time they shouted and beat upon the door, but no one came. Finally Barda charged at the door in fury, trying to burst it with his shoulder, but the wood was thick, the lock was heavy, and his efforts were of no use.

At last they admitted defeat and flung themselves back on their beds.

"We were fools not to expect this," Barda panted.

Jasmine was silent. Lief knew that she was fighting panic. For Jasmine, being imprisoned was the worst sort of torture. After a moment she sprang to her feet and ran to the window, shaking the bars and calling loudly to the blank sky. But the wind snatched her cries and blew them away unheard.

"Could Kree fit through the bars?" asked Lief. Jasmine shook her head, but the question had given her an idea. She snatched the cover from her bed and pushed it halfway through the bars so that it flapped in the breeze like a flag.

The second bell rang. Time dragged on. Lief gritted his teeth. How their enemy must be laughing at the ease with which they had been tricked.

Suddenly there was a sharp knock at the door and the handle rattled. They all shouted and immediately heard the sound of a key in the lock. The door swung open to reveal Mother Brightly, wearing a bright red dress and a sunbonnet tied with green and blue ribbons. Her cheeks were flushed and she was very short of breath.

"I was just leaving for the Games when what did I see but one of my coverlets flapping from a window!" she exclaimed. "I could not believe my eyes, and came running at once."

Quickly Lief, Barda, and Jasmine explained what had happened. The woman listened with many exclamations of horror and dismay.

"Oh, I am ashamed that this has happened at my inn!" she cried. "I hope the upset will not affect your performance. I have told everyone that I think you will be finalists, at least."

"But — is it not too late?" Lief asked.

Mother Brightly shook her head decidedly. "Not at all!" she snapped. "Follow me."

Leaving Kree and Filli behind in the room, Lief, Barda, and Jasmine followed the woman down the stairs to the empty dining hall. There she served them food, and great mugs of foaming Queen Bee Cider. "Eat and be strong," she said fiercely. "We will show your spiteful enemy that Mother Brightly's favorites are not to be trifled with!"

When they had eaten and drunk their fill, she led them through the training rooms at the back of the inn, along a covered walkway, and into an arena. The Games Opening Ceremony was still in progress, and many heads turned to look at the newcomers. Barda, Jasmine, and Lief lifted their chins and ignored the stares and whispers.

"Good fortune!" Mother Brightly whispered, and bustled away, leaving the companions alone.

The arena was a large, round field of sand surrounded by rows of benches that rose, tier after tier, high into the air. The benches were crowded with people, many of them waving red, green, and blue flags bearing the gold medal that was the symbol of the Games.

The competitors, clustered together on the sand, raised their hands, pledging that they would fight as well as they were able. Among them, easily seen because they were so tall, stood Joanna and Orwen. The scar-faced stranger was there also, not far from where Lief was standing. A ragged piece of cloth was knotted around his neck like a scarf.

Was it protection from the sun? Or to hide a wound made by Jasmine's dagger in the hallway last night? Lief's fist clenched as he raised his own hand. All his doubts and fears had disappeared. Now he was only angry, and determined to show that he could not be defeated so easily.

✳

Soon afterwards, pairs of names were read out, and the contests began. The rules were simple. All the pairs fought at one time. Each pair fought until one could no longer stand.

The loser was taken away. The winner, after only a few minutes' rest, was paired with another winner to fight again, for endurance was considered as important as strength, agility, speed, and cunning.

Lief, Barda, and Jasmine soon learned that the idea of a fair contest played no part in the Rithmere Games. Competitors fought with savage fury, biting and clawing, butting with their heads and tearing at their rivals' hair and eyes, as well as punching and kicking. Nothing was forbidden except the use of weapons.

The crowd roared, waving their flags, urging their favorites on, hissing and booing those who did not fight well. Sellers of sweetmeats, hot food, and Queen Bee Cider did a fine trade as they wandered up and down the aisles between the seats, shouting their wares.

As more and more defeated competitors left the arena, disappointed and nursing their injuries, the space between the struggling pairs grew greater. Each fight was harder than the last, but Lief, Barda, and Jasmine managed to survive every round.

Unlike most of their rivals they were used to

fighting for their lives. They had all learned much since they first met in the Forests of Silence. But even their early training helped them now.

Not for nothing had Lief spent his childhood on the dangerous streets of Del. As Barda had told Mother Brightly, he could dodge and run with the best, and use his wits to foil enemies far bigger than himself. He was young, but because of his work with his father in the blacksmith's forge his body was strong, his muscles used to working hard.

From boyhood Barda had trained as a palace guard — and the guards were the most powerful fighters in Deltora, only defeated at last by the sorcery of the Shadow Lord. For many years Barda had wrestled and fought his fellows as part of that training. And even during his time disguised as a beggar outside the forge gates he had kept his strength, following Lief through the city and protecting him from harm.

And Jasmine? Small and slight as she was, no one in that company had faced what she had faced, or lived the life that she had lived. Shrewd Mother Brightly had seen the strength in those slim arms, and the determination in the green eyes. But Jasmine's opponents continually mistook her smallness for weakness, and paid the price.

✳

The sun was low in the sky when the eight finalists, the ones who would fight their last battles on the morrow, were announced.

Barda, Lief, and Jasmine were among them. So were Joanna and Orwen. The other three were a short, heavily muscled man called Glock, a woman, Neridah, whose speed had amazed the crowd, and the scar-faced stranger whose name the companions now learned for the first time — Doom.

"A fitting name for such a dark character," muttered Barda, as Doom stepped forward, unsmiling, and held up his arms to the cheering crowd. "I do not relish the idea of fighting him."

Neither did Lief. But he had thought of something that worried him even more. "I did not expect that we would all be finalists," he whispered. "What if we have to fight each other?"

Jasmine stared at him. "Why, we will decide who is to win, then just pretend to fight," she said. "As, in any case, we must do for all our other bouts tomorrow. We must let our opponents win, and so avoid injury. We are already sure of 100 gold coins each, because we are finalists. That is all the money we need, and more."

Barda moved restlessly. Plainly, the idea of cheating to lose offended him as much as the idea of cheating to win. "It would not be honorable . . ." he began.

"Not *honorable*?" hissed Jasmine. "What has *honor* to do with this?" She spun around to Lief. "Tell him!" she urged.

Lief hesitated. He was not troubled, as Barda was, by the idea of deceiving the organizers of the

Games, or even the crowd. On the streets of Del, honor among friends was all that was required, and survival was the only rule. But part of his mind — the part that still simmered with anger over the warning note and the locked door — rebelled against Jasmine's plan.

"Our rivals will know, if we do not try to win. It will seem that we are at last bowing to their threats," he said in a low voice.

Jasmine snorted in disgust. "You are as foolish as Barda! Will you risk our quest for the sake of your pride? Oh, I have no patience with you!"

She turned her back and stalked away.

*

That evening the finalists ate together in the dining hall attended by Mother Brightly, smiling and bright in her ruffled red dress. It was a strange meal, for where only the night before the room had been busy and filled with noise, now it was empty and echoing. The defeated competitors, it seemed, had already been sent away. Lief wondered how they were faring, for many of them were injured and almost all without money.

Jasmine was still angry. She ate little and drank only water. "That Queen Bee Cider is too rich for me," she muttered. "The thought of it sickens me. The air in the arena stank of it. The people in the seats were drinking it all day."

Barda frowned. "It should not be sold to them. It

is intended for use by fighters, who need massive energy, not for those who simply sit and look on. No wonder they cry for blood."

Just then Mother Brightly rang a small bell.

"One word before you begin retiring to your rooms, my dears," she said, as all the finalists turned to her. "I want no tricks or trouble here tonight, so I plan to take your keys and lock your doors myself. I will unlock them in the morning immediately after the waking bell."

There was complete silence in the room. The woman looked around, her plump face very serious. "So sleep soundly and regain your strength," she went on. "Tomorrow you must show no sign of weakness or lack of purpose. The crowd — well, it is always very excited on the final day. Very excited, indeed. It has been known for finalists who do not perform well to be attacked and torn to pieces. I would not like this to happen to any of you."

Lief's stomach seemed to turn over. He did not dare glance at Jasmine or Barda. So this was how the Games organizers made sure that all the finalists tried their best at the last. The crowd was their weapon — the crowd, swarming, acting with one mind, excited to fever pitch and hungry for blood.

9 - The Finalists

The arena was already growing warm when they reached it in the morning. The sun glared down on one side of the newly raked sand. The other side was in deep shadow. The benches were packed, the crowd simmering with excitement.

The eight finalists raised their hands and re-peated their pledge to fight their best. Then they stepped forward one by one to choose a card from the woven basket held up by a smiling Mother Brightly.

Lief looked at his card, his heart in his mouth. The number upon it was 3. He glanced at Barda and Jasmine and to his relief saw that Barda was holding up number 1, and Jasmine number 4. So, for this round at least, they were not to fight each other. But who were their opponents to be?

He looked around and his heart sank as he saw scar-faced Doom walking towards Barda, holding his card high so that all could see the number 1 upon it. The giant Orwen had drawn the second number 4 and was already standing with Jasmine, who looked like a child beside him. Glock and Joanna had both drawn cards marked 2. So the only one who remained was Neridah the Swift. And, sure enough, there she was, hurrying towards him showing the 3 card that proved she was paired with him.

The crowd roared as the four pairs of opponents threw down their cards and faced each other.

Neridah looked down at her hands, then up at Lief. "I am rather afraid, I confess," she said in a low voice. "I really do not know how I reached the finals. And you are one of Mother Brightly's favorites, are you not?"

Lief stared awkwardly back at her. He had fought several women the day before, and had learned that it was unwise to think of them as anything other than dangerous opponents. Besides, anyone who had seen Jasmine at work knew better than to underestimate a fighter just because she was female. But Neridah looked so gentle. She was as tall as he was, but slender and graceful as a deer, with a deer's huge, dark eyes.

"The . . . the crowd," he stammered. "We must . . ."

"Of course!" Neridah whispered. "I know I must try my very hardest. And I will not blame you for doing what you must. Whatever happens to me, my poor sisters and my mother will have the 100 gold coins I have already won. Mother Brightly has promised."

"You need not fear . . ." Lief began gently. But at that moment the starting bell rang, and like a snake, Neridah's foot lashed out and caught him on the point of the chin, knocking him flat on his back.

The crowd laughed and booed.

Lief scrambled to his feet, shaking his head stupidly. His ears were ringing. He could not see Neridah at all. With amazing speed she had darted behind him. Savagely she kicked the backs of his knees, and he stumbled forward, gasping in pain. In moments she was darting around him, leaping and kicking at his ankles, his knees, his belly, his back, making him turn around and around like a confused clown, flailing with his arms while always she stayed out of reach.

She was making a fool of him! The crowd had begun jeering, chanting his stupid false name, "Twig," and laughing. A wave of anger cleared Lief's head a little. If Neridah was fast, so was he. He jumped backwards, away from her, so that she was forced to face him. Warily, they circled one another. Then, without warning he sprang forward, catching her around the waist and throwing her to the ground.

She fell and lay gasping, one arm limp and helpless. All Lief had to do was finish her. Stop her from rising to her feet. Kick, or hit . . .

But tears were welling from her eyes as she struggled feebly in the sand. "Please . . ." she whispered.

For one split second, Lief hesitated. And that was enough. The next moment Neridah's "helpless" arm was darting forward and her hand was seizing his ankle. Then the crowd was roaring as she leaped up, jerking his foot off the ground. Lief staggered, crashed to the sand, and knew no more.

✳

Meanwhile, Barda and Doom were wrestling, trying to push each other over. They were very evenly matched. Barda was taller, but Doom's muscles were like iron and his will even stronger. From side to side, back and forth, the two men swayed, but neither made a mistake, and neither gave in.

Wherever you have come from, Doom of the Hills, you have had a life of struggle, thought Barda. You have suffered much. And he remembered the sign that the scar-faced man had made in the dust of a shop counter, the first time he had seen him. The sign of the Resistance. The secret sign of those who were pledged to defy the Shadow Lord.

"What are you doing here, Doom?" he panted. "Why do you waste your time fighting me when you have more important work to do?"

"What work?" hissed Doom, the long scar showing white on his gleaming skin. "My work — now — is to grind you into the dust — Berry of Bushtown!"

His lips twisted into a grim smile as he said the name. Plainly he was sure that it was false.

"Your friend Twig is down and will not get up again," he sneered. "See, behind you? Hear the crowd?"

Barda struggled to keep his concentration, refusing to look around, trying to close his ears to the howls of the people. Yet he could still hear the frenzied chanting: "Neridah! Neridah! Kick! Yes! Again! Finish him!"

Doom's grip tightened and his weight shifted. Barda staggered, but only a little. "Not so easy, Doom!" he muttered. He gritted his teeth and fought on.

✳

Jasmine could see nothing but Orwen's huge shape circling her, hear nothing but his savage grunts as he lunged for her, and the beating of her own heart as she sprang aside. Her mind was working as fast as her feet.

All the competitors she had fought the day before had been larger than she was, but none of them had been Orwen's size and weight. If she allowed herself to be caught in this giant's bear-like grip, he would crush her. She knew she had to be like a bee buzzing around the head of a great beast. She had to irritate him, tire him, so that he made a mistake.

But Orwen was not stupid. He knew what she planned. For a very long time she had kept out of his reach, spinning and jumping, landing sharp, painful little kicks on his ankles and knees. His face was running with sweat, but his steady gaze had not faltered.

Again she leaped away from him. For long minutes she had been trying to turn him to face the sun. And she had nearly done it. One or two more moves . . .

Then, suddenly, Orwen's expression changed. He was looking over Jasmine's shoulder, his eyes filled with horror. Was it a trick? Or . . .

Behind her there was a terrible sound — the sound of someone choking, in agony. And the crowd was roaring: "Glock! Glock! Kill! Kill! Kill!"

Orwen lunged forward. Jasmine darted aside, but almost immediately realized that the man was not looking at her. He had forgotten she was there.

Joanna was down, pinned to the ground. And Glock was kneeling over her, his huge, hairy hands gripping her neck, shaking, tightening, his teeth bared in savage glee as he watched her life ebb away.

Then Orwen was upon him, heaving him aside like a bundle of rags. The watching people shrieked with excitement. Glock's snarl of shock and fury was cut short as he thumped heavily to the ground. Orwen threw himself down beside Joanna, cradling her in his arms.

She was so limp and still that Jasmine thought at first that she was dead. But as Orwen called her name, her eyelids flickered and her hand fumbled towards her bruised throat. Orwen bent his head with a groan of relief, unconscious of everything but her.

And so it was that he did not sense Glock staggering to his feet and coming for him. He did not hear Jasmine's sharp, warning cry. He paid no heed to the crowd rising in a fever of excitement. The next moment, Glock's locked, clenched fists had pounded down onto the back of his neck like two great stones. Orwen fell forward without a cry, and did not move again.

✳

Barda and Doom were still fighting, struggling in a grip that neither would break. They were alone in the arena now. Dimly, Barda was aware that two people had been carried away while Glock, held back by three strong officials, still raved at them with murderous rage.

"Glock is a madman!" Doom growled. His voice was full of loathing.

"And are *we* not madmen?" panted Barda. "Whichever one of us wins will surely have to fight him. Do you want 1000 gold coins enough for that?"

"Do *you*?" hissed Doom, his dark eyes flashing. "For my own purposes I am condemned to this. But you — surely you are not. We have given a good enough show. If one of us falls now, he is free to go on his way. Think!"

Barda thought, and faltered.

It was the smallest hesitation. One tiny gap in

the concentration that had armored him for so long. But it was enough for Doom. A twist, a mighty thrust, and Barda was off balance and staggering.

The other man's fist crashed into his jaw. Barda saw bright pinpoints of light. Then the ground was rushing up to meet him. In seconds he was lying on his face in the sand, dazed, his head spinning, his whole body aching, listening to the crowd howling Doom's name. Through his pain he wondered if Doom had tricked him, or done him a great favor. Had this defeat been because of Doom's wish, or his own?

10 - The Champion

Four finalists remained: Neridah, Doom, Glock — and Jasmine, for she had been pronounced the winner of her bout, even though Orwen had been felled by another.

Jasmine had only had a few brief moments to find out how Lief and Barda were faring. Both were poorly, but Mother Brightly, anxiously hovering over them, had told her that, like Joanna and Orwen, they would soon recover. Their injuries were not too serious, and they would be not much the worse for their defeat.

Seeing that her friends were in good hands, Jasmine allowed herself to be taken to the center of the arena to join Glock, Neridah, and Doom.

Foaming mugs of Queen Bee Cider were brought to them. The dark-haired young serving man was plainly excited to be serving such great ones. He offered the tray to Doom, who took a mug with a word of thanks.

"Why do you serve him first?" shouted Glock furiously. He snatched another mug from the tray, tipped it up, and drained it dry.

The young man, plainly startled and frightened, began gasping words of apology.

"All is well," said Doom quietly. "Do not upset yourself."

Blushing scarlet, the young man held out the tray to Neridah and Jasmine. Neridah took a mug and drank it in a gulp. Jasmine, however, shook her head.

"Thank you, but I do not like Queen Bee Cider," she said. "I have had water, and that is enough."

As the young man stared, Glock grabbed the rejected mug. "All the more for me!" he crowed, gulping the cider greedily.

He turned to Jasmine, wiping his dripping mouth with the back of his hand. "Pray that you are not facing me next round, little water-drinking Birdie. I will crack your bones like eggshells. I will . . ."

A strange expression crossed his face. And at that exact moment, Neridah, beside him, gave a strange little sigh, bent at the knees, and fell to the ground. Glock gaped at her, then at the empty mug in his hand. His hand went to his throat.

"Poison!" he croaked. He turned, staggering, and pointed with a shaking finger at the young man with the tray. "You — " he croaked.

The young man dropped the tray and took to his heels. By the time Glock, in his turn, had crashed senseless to the ground, he was already lost in the crowd.

People were running towards them, shouting and pointing. Jasmine stared at Doom.

"This is your doing!" she hissed. "That boy — you knew him!"

"What rubbish you talk," he snapped.

Jasmine narrowed her eyes. "You think that if the others are out of the way — if you fight only me in the finals — you will surely win," she said slowly. "But you are wrong, Doom."

He turned away so that she could not see his face. The officials had reached them now. They were shaking Glock and Neridah, gabbling and exclaiming. Only Jasmine heard Doom's reply.

"We will see," he said softly. "We will see."

✳

If fighting Orwen was like fighting a bear, this is like facing a wolf, Jasmine thought, as she and Doom circled each other in the center of the arena. A lean, cunning wolf.

The man was dangerous. Very dangerous. Her every instinct told her that. She feared him as she had never feared a human being before, yet she did not know why. She searched for a reason, then thought she had found it.

He does not care if he lives or dies, she thought,

and despite herself she shivered with dread. She saw a tiny spark leap into Doom's eyes and dodged just in time as he lunged for her.

The crowd, cheated of the semifinal contests and angry because their favorite, Glock, could not fight again, was in an ugly mood. A roar of boos and shouted curses rose up as Doom missed his prey by a breath. They were tired of this circling and dodging. They wanted action. They wanted blood.

Breathing hard, Jasmine whirled to face her enemy again. His mouth twisted into a mocking smile. "Where is your boasting now, little bird?" he jeered softly. "Why, you cannot master your fear enough even to put up a good show for the crowd. Run home and hide your head in your mamma's lap!"

A flame of white-hot anger ran through Jasmine's body, burning away the fear. She looked up at Doom, and with satisfaction saw the smile fade as he sensed the change in her. She saw his mouth tense, and a wary look creep into his eyes.

"You are tired, old man," she hissed. "Tired to your bones."

And as she said it, she knew that it was true. His long struggle with Barda had sapped his strength and dulled his reflexes. Why else had he missed her when he struck?

"Catch me if you can!" she grinned, and half-turned as if to run.

Taken by surprise, Doom took a stumbling step

forward. She whirled around and kicked, whirled and kicked once more. She leaped away from him as he snatched at her, leaving him clutching the empty air. She jumped and attacked again and again.

With savage pleasure she heard his grunts of pain and anger, heard the crowd begin to cheer. Their excitement was mounting-and so was hers. The game went on and on. Doom could not touch her.

The arena was a blur. She felt nothing but her own desire to punish and hurt. It was as though her blood was bubbling, as though her anger had turned into energy, surging around her body, making her feet and hands tingle. Laughing, she danced backwards as Doom came at her again, tall and glowering. The crowd howled. The roar was deafening. So loud . . . why was it so loud . . . ?

She stepped back — and her heel hit solid wood.

She glanced behind her in shock and saw a wall, and above it, a mass of red, shouting faces. Only then did she realize how she had been tricked, how foolish her anger had made her. Little by little, Doom had pushed her to the edge of the arena. She had her back to the low wall that surrounded it. And he was closing in on her.

She sprang up, up and back, landing surefooted on the top of the wall as so many times she had landed on tree branches in the Forests of Silence. Behind her the crowd was screaming. But Doom was close, very close, leaning forward, and his hands were reaching for her ankles. Hands like giant spiders. Arms like thick, hungry vines . . .

Pure instinct drove her to jump, to spring up and out towards him. For a split second his bent shoulders were her tree branch. Then she had thrust backward with her feet, launching herself into the air once more, sending him toppling forward. She heard him cry out, heard him fall crashing against the wall as she turned in the air and landed lightly on the sand far behind him.

She landed poised to run. Her only thought had been to escape. But her leap for freedom had done far more than that.

Doom lay crumpled by the wall, unmoving. The crowd was on its feet, shrieking her name. Slowly, in wonderment, Jasmine realized that the fight was over. She had won.

✳

"So — it is all over for another year! And what a thrilling contest our final was at the last!" laughed Mother Brightly, as she hurried Lief, Barda, and Jasmine back to the inn after the presentation ceremony. "A little slow to start, perhaps. But then the fun began!"

She patted Jasmine's shoulder affectionately. "You are a popular Champion, my dear. There is nothing the crowd likes better than agility beating strength."

Jasmine was silent. The gold medallion hung

heavy around her neck. A bag of gold coins was heavy in her arms. And her heart was heavier than both.

She felt sick at the thought of what she had become for a short time in that arena. A beast who took pleasure in hurting and punishing another. A fool who forgot everything in the heady delight of battle. She had been as vicious as the loathsome Glock. As drunk with violence as that reeking, bellowing crowd. If her conceit had been her undoing, as it so nearly had, it would have served her right.

Lief and Barda glanced at one another over her head. They knew her well enough to guess a little of what she was feeling. But Mother Brightly could not imagine that Jasmine was anything but proud.

"To tell you the truth," she chattered on, lowering her voice, "I was very pleased to see that person Doom brought down. A proud and glowering man — with an unpleasant past, I am sure. I am certain that it was he who arranged for the cider to be drugged. He skulked away, you know, as soon as he woke, not even waiting for his 100 gold coins. Surely this shows that he has a guilty conscience."

"Have Glock and Neridah woken?" asked Lief.

Mother Brightly shook her head sadly. "They still sleep like babes," she sighed. "They will not be able to leave here till tomorrow. But Joanna and Orwen have left already. Joanna was limping badly and Orwen's head had a nasty lump, but they would not be persuaded to remain." She sighed again. "It seems that having gotten their hands on the gold they had no further use for Rithmere."

Lief had no desire to stay any longer than he had to either, and plainly Barda agreed.

"Sadly, we must hurry away, too, Mother Brightly," the big man said tactfully, as they moved into the inn. "But we need to buy some supplies before we leave. Can you recommend — ?"

"Why, I have everything you need!" Mother Brightly interrupted. "I sell all manner of travellers' supplies."

And so it proved. As soon as they had fetched Kree and Filli from their room, the companions went with Mother Brightly to a storeroom stacked to the roof with packs, sleeping blankets, water bottles, ropes, fire chips, dried food, and dozens of other useful items.

As Lief, Barda, and Jasmine had suspected, everything was very expensive. But they had plenty of gold to spend and, like other winners before them, they were happy to pay more so as not to have to wander the town. Within half an hour they had everything they needed. Then, at Mother Brightly's insistence, they ate for the last time in the empty dining hall.

Lief did not enjoy the meal. He was plagued by the uncomfortable feeling that all was not as it should be. His skin kept prickling, as though they were being spied upon. Yet who could be watching them? Neridah and Glock were still asleep. Joanna, Orwen, and Doom had left.

He shrugged the feeling off, telling himself that he was being foolish.

11 - Easy as Winking

Mother Brightly was in high spirits all the time they were eating, but afterwards, when she had brought their weapons to them and they were preparing to leave, it became clear that something was on her mind.

In the end, she bit her lip and bent towards them. "It is hard for me to say this," she said in a low voice. "I do not like to spread bad tidings about the Games, or Rithmere. But — you must be told. It has been known for Champions, and even ordinary finalists, to meet with . . . ill fortune, on their way out of the town."

"You mean they are attacked and robbed?" asked Barda bluntly.

Mother Brightly nodded uncomfortably. "The gold coins are a great temptation," she murmured. "Would you be offended if I suggested that you leave

81

the inn by a secret way? There is a back door —
reached by a passage that runs from the cellar. The
cider barrels are brought in that way, but few people
know of it, and the back street is narrow, and always
deserted. You could slip out unseen, easy as winking."

"Thank you, Mother Brightly," said Lief, clasp-
ing her hand warmly. "You are a good friend."

✳

The passage from the cellar was long, low, and dark
and smelled sickeningly of cider. Their boots clattered
on the stones as they shuffled along in single file,
Barda bent almost double. They had divided their re-
maining gold between them, to make it easier to carry,
but still it weighed heavily on their belts. Already sore
from their battles of the day, they were soon very stiff
and uncomfortable.

"We should, perhaps, have stayed the night at
the inn and set out in the morning," groaned Lief.
"But I could not face the thought of one more hour in
Rithmere."

"Nor I," muttered Jasmine, breaking her long silence. Kree, hunched on her arm, squawked agree-
ment.

"At least we have what we came for," said
Barda, who was in the lead. "We now have enough
gold to fund the rest of our journey — and more besides." He paused, then added awkwardly: "You did
well, Jasmine."

"Indeed," Lief agreed eagerly.

"I did not do well," Jasmine said in a low voice. "I am ashamed. The man Doom jeered about my mother. He made me angry. He *meant* to do it. He wanted me to forget myself — so I would perform for the crowd."

"He tricked himself, then," said Barda. "For in the end he lost and you won. Think of that, and forget the rest." He paused, and pointed. "I see light ahead. I think we are at last reaching the end of this accursed tunnel."

They hurried forward, eager to see the sun and to stand upright.

As Mother Brightly had told them, the passage ended in a low door. Light showed dimly through the crack beneath it. But as Barda drew the bolt, and the door swung open, a flood of sunlight poured into the passage.

With streaming eyes, almost blinded by the welcome glare, they crawled through the doorway one by one. And so it was that, one by one, they were cracked over the head and captured. Easy as winking.

✳

When Lief came to his senses he was covered by some rough, foul-smelling cloth — old sacks, perhaps. His head was pounding. He was gagged, and his wrists and ankles were weighed down by heavy chains.

He became aware that he was being painfully

jolted and bumped. He could hear voices, a jingling sound, and the plod of hooves. He realized that he was on the back of a cart. Whoever had attacked him was carrying him away from Rithmere. But why?

The Belt!

With a thrill of terror he dragged his chained hands to his waist and groaned with relief as his fingers met the familiar shape of the linked medallions under his clothes. His money bag was gone. His sword, too. But the Belt of Deltora was safe. His captors had not found it. Yet.

His groan was answered by the dull clank of chains and a sigh beside him and a muffled cry from a little farther away. So Barda and Jasmine were in the cart with him. He was absurdly comforted, though of course it would have been better if one of them at least was free. Then there might be some hope of rescue. As it was . . .

There was a guffawing laugh from the front of the cart. "The ticks are waking, Carn 8," a harsh voice said. "Will I give them another knock?"

"Better not," said a second voice. "They have to be in good condition on delivery."

"I don't see that this lot's worth the trouble," the first man growled. "The big one might be all right, but the other two are rubbish! Especially the scrawny little female. Champion my eye! She won't last five minutes in the Shadow Arena."

Lief lay rigid, straining his ears to hear more

against the sound of rain, fighting down a feeling of dread.

"It's not our business to say what's worth the trouble, Carn 2," answered the other voice. "It's the old girl who answers to the Master, not us. The pod was told that from the beginning. The Brightly woman supplies the goods. All we have to do is deliver them undamaged."

Lief felt the blood rush to his head. Beside him, Barda made a strangled sound.

"The ticks heard us," sniggered the man the other had called Carn 2.

"What does it matter? They're not going to be telling anyone, are they?" sneered his companion. "Or d'you think that black bird's going to spread the word? It's still there, you know. Right behind us."

They laughed, and the cart jolted on.

＊

The journey continued hour after hour. Lief slept and woke and slept again. It grew colder and darker, and then it started to rain again. The sacks that covered him became sodden. He began to shiver.

"We'd better stop and get the ticks covered up," Carn 8 growled at last. "Give them some grub and a drink, as well, or they'll be dying on us. Then we'll be in the muck."

The cart jolted off the road, and finally came to a stop. The next Lief knew he was being hauled out of the cart and dumped roughly onto the ground. Agonizing pain shot through his head and he moaned aloud. Only the cold rain beating on his face kept him conscious.

"Be careful, you fool!" roared Carn 8. "How many times do you have to be told? Any broken bones Brightly didn't put in her report and we're in the Arena ourselves! Do you want to end your days in gladiators' leather, fighting a Vraal? Get him under the canopy, and be quick about it!"

The other grumbled. His face and shoulders loomed out of the darkness as he bent and grabbed Lief under the arms. And it was then that Lief's worst suspicions were confirmed. Their captors were Grey Guards.

✳

The Guards had made a rough shelter for their prisoners by stretching oiled cloth between the lowest branches of a tree. Barda, Jasmine, and Lief huddled together under this canopy, shuddering with cold.

Kree, who had followed them all the way from Rithmere, perched on Jasmine's shoulder. But he could not help them. There was no chance of escape. Their leg irons were fixed to an iron peg driven into the ground.

The gags were taken off and they were given water and some chunks of bread. Then the Guards moved away. Dimly, through the darkness and the rain, Lief saw them crawl together under the cart where it seemed they were planning to sleep.

"I cannot eat weighed down by these chains," Jasmine shouted.

"Hold your tongue or I'll cut it out and throw you into the Shifting Sands, orders or no!" bawled Carn 2. "We passed by the Sands just an hour ago."

"Lief, is the Belt safe?" whispered Barda.

"Yes," Lief whispered back. "Did you hear — ?"

"Yes. We are not far from the Shifting Sands. But this news is of little use to us as we are. Mother Brightly fooled us well."

"I thought *she* was the fool," Jasmine hissed bitterly, breaking off a tiny piece of bread for Filli. "But the secret way out of the inn was a trap."

"The whole of the Games is a trap! With gold coins as bait." Lief clenched his fists. "What better way to lure the best and strongest fighters, and make them show how good they are? And dear old Mother Brightly is there all the time, to make sure that as many finalists as possible walk tamely into captivity when it is all over."

Barda shook his head in disgust. "We heard on the highway that few Games Champions are ever heard of again. Now we know why. They do not run away to spend their money in peace. They are taken to the Shadowlands to die battling wild beasts and each other for the amusement of the crowds."

"And their gold coins, and even the Champion medallion, are taken to be used again!" Jasmine hissed. "It is monstrous."

The rain eased, and they heard snores coming from beneath the cart. The Guards were asleep. With new urgency they began struggling to free themselves, though in their hearts they all knew that it was no use.

They had long given up their efforts and were dozing fitfully when Kree gave a startled squawk and there was the tiny sound of cracking twigs behind them.

"Be still!" breathed a voice. "Do not speak or move until I tell you. I already have your packs and weapons in a safe place. Now I am going to unlock your chains. When you are free, follow me as quietly as you can!"

12 – No Choice

A short time afterwards, astounded by their unexpected release, the three companions sat back on their heels in the shelter of a cave and stared in amazement at their rescuer: Doom.

Impatiently, he waved away their thanks.

"Listen carefully," he said. "We have little time. I am the leader of a group sworn to resist the Shadow Lord. We have been suspicious of the Games for some time — certain that they were not all they seemed. My purpose there was to see what was happening, from the inside. Your presence upset my plans. I tried to scare you off — "

"It was you who locked us in our room!" Lief broke in. "You who attacked us."

"Yes — and got cut for my pains." Doom grimaced, touching the cloth at his neck. "I was trying to stop you from competing — to protect you."

"Why?" Barda asked bluntly.

"When first I saw you in Tom's shop something about you interested me. I was hurrying on business of my own and could not stay. But ever since, wherever I have been, I have heard whispers about three travellers — a man, a boy, and a wild girl, accompanied by a black bird. Wherever these travellers go, it is said, part of the Shadow Lord's evil is undone."

Lief gripped Barda's arm. If word about them was spreading, how long would it be before the Shadow Lord became aware of them?

But Jasmine, who still could not make up her mind to trust Doom, had something else on her mind. "You allowed us to be captured," she accused. "You crept away after the finals, but you did not leave. You hid in the inn, watched, and did not lift a hand to help us."

Doom shrugged. "I had no choice. I had to find out how the trick was worked. I had intended that animal Glock to be proclaimed Champion, and suffer whatever fate was in store for him. But he took the drugged drink intended for you, girl, and instead of losing to him, as I had planned, I had to find a way of pretending to lose to you."

Jasmine drew herself up. "You played your part well," she said coldly. "In fact, I would have sworn that you *did* lose. Or am I mistaken in thinking you hit your head on the wall, and slid down it almost unconscious?"

Doom's grim face relaxed into a half smile. "You will never know, will you?" he said dryly.

"If it had been Glock who had been captured, would you have rescued him?" asked Lief curiously.

The smile disappeared. "You ask too many questions," growled Doom. "What is certain is that I must save him now, for he and the woman Neridah will be following in your footsteps tomorrow, and I cannot release one without the other. It is unfortunate."

He stared broodingly out into the rain for a moment, then turned to them again. "A group is waiting not far away. Among them is Dain, the boy who helped me at the Games. He will lead you into the mountains where we have a stronghold. You will be safe there."

Barda, Lief, and Jasmine glanced at one another.

"We are grateful to you," said Barda at last. "And I hope you will not take this amiss. But I fear we cannot accept your offer. We must continue our travels. There is — something of importance we must do."

Doom frowned. "Whatever it is, you must abandon it for now," he said. "I could not risk trying to kill the Guards. It was dangerous enough stealing your weapons and supplies from the cart while they slept below."

"They have our gold, I think," sighed Lief.

"Yes, I saw them take it," Doom said. "But their master will care nothing for that. It is you he wants. When they wake and find you gone they will track you wherever you go. They will not rest until you are found."

"All the better, then, that we do not lead them to your stronghold," said Barda calmly. He put on his sword and pack and began crawling from the cave. Doom put a hand on his shoulder to stop him.

"We are many, and at our base we have ways of dealing with Guards," he said. "You had better join us. What could be more important than our cause? What is this mysterious mission that cannot wait?"

Barda, unsmiling, pulled the restraining hand from his shoulder and continued crawling from the cave. Jasmine and Lief followed. Outside, the rain still fell and the sky was black and starless.

Doom appeared beside them, silent as a shadow. "Go your way, then," he said, his voice very cold. "But say nothing to anyone of what I have told you this night, or you will wish you had gone to the Shadow-lands."

Without another word, he disappeared into the dripping bushes, and was gone.

"How dare he threaten us!" hissed Jasmine.

"He is angry." Lief felt very low-spirited. His head ached, he was cold, and he was sorry to have parted with Doom on bad terms. "I think he is a man who rarely trusts. Yet he trusted us. Now he fears that he was foolish to do so, for we would not trust him in return."

Barda nodded slowly. "I wish it could have been otherwise," he said. "He would have been a valuable ally. But we could not risk it. Doom would not be content to let us keep our secret. And there are spies everywhere — even his band may not be safe. Later, if we succeed in our quest — "

Kree squawked impatiently.

"We will not live to succeed in anything if we do not move on," Jasmine said. "It is nearly dawn."

"But which way do we go?" Lief looked around him in frustration. "We have no idea where we are, and we do not even have the stars to guide us."

"You are forgetting Kree," Jasmine smiled. "He followed us. He knows exactly where we are."

They began to walk, Kree fluttering ahead of them. Soon they found a tiny stream which had been swelled by the rain. They plunged into it and splashed along its bed for as long as they could, hoping that the water would disguise their scent.

All of them felt bruised and ill and longed to rest. But the thought of the Grey Guards following them like evil tracking dogs drove them on.

Dawn came, and with it the sun, struggling feebly through the clouds. Soon afterwards they reached a narrow road heavily marked by puddled cart tracks. On the other side of the road was a wooden fence and beyond that a stretch of stony land ending at a row of low grey hills. Kree flew to a fence post and flapped his wings impatiently, hopping to the left.

"If we walk along the fence, we will at least leave no tracks," murmured Jasmine. "Hurry!"

Gathering themselves for the effort, they leaped across the road, climbed the fence, and began moving along it, Jasmine balancing on the top, and Barda and Lief edging uncomfortably along with their feet on the middle rail.

After a short time they reached a crossroads. The fence continued around the corner and on into the distance where it was lost in the grey hills. And right beside the corner post stood a huge, weathered stone. It was as tall as Lief. Words had been carved on it, but so long ago that many of the letters had disappeared.

```
TH  S   I  T  G SA    S

    DA  G  R!

DEA H SW   MS WI   IN ITS ROC  Y WALL
W  ERE ALL A  E ONE, O  E WILL  ULES  LL.
BE  OW TH   DE  D, THE LIV NG STRIVE
WITH MINDLE  S WILL TO  S  V      IVE.
```

"The Shifting Sands. Danger!" Barda squinted at the stone. "That much I can make out, but what the smaller writing says I cannot say. Too many of the letters have been worn away by wind and weather."

"I think the first word is 'Death,' " said Lief in a low voice. He leaned out from the fence and touched the stone, tracing the letters with the tips of his fingers. Hesitantly, using touch as well as sight, he began to read.

"Death swarms within its rocky wall,
Where all are one, one will rules all . . ."

"Go on, Lief!" Jasmine urged, as he paused.

Lief shook his head, frowning. "The next two lines are more worn than the others. They seem to say something like: 'Be now the dead, the living strive . . . With mindless will to survive.' But that does not really make sense."

"It makes enough sense to tell us that the Sands are not going to be pleasant," said Barda dryly. "But we knew that, I think."

Jasmine's mind was busy with practical matters. "Since the verse talks of a 'rocky wall' I would guess that the Sands are just beyond the hills. But we will have to cross the plain to reach them. The stones may hide our tracks, but there will be no way to disguise our scent."

"It cannot be helped," said Lief. He climbed over the fence and jumped gratefully to the ground on the other side, flexing his cramped fingers. "Besides, we have been very careful. The Guards have surely lost our trail by now."

"I would not count on that," muttered Barda. But he also climbed to the ground and after a moment Jasmine jumped down to join them. They set off, almost running over the bare ground, glancing often behind them. Despite his hopeful words, Lief looked back as often as his companions did. The idea of Grey Guards silently following, the idea of a deadly blister flying unseen towards him to explode on his back, made his skin crawl.

It became warmer as the sun climbed steadily behind its veil of cloud, and steam began to rise from the wet ground. The grey hills ahead were also quickly shrouded in mist. So it was only when the companions actually reached them that they realized that these were not ordinary hills at all, but thousands of huge boulders heaped together to make a high, natural wall — the "rocky wall" of the verse.

They began to climb and soon lost all sight of the ground below. Everything around them was white. The air grew thick and all sound was dulled. Cautiously, one step at a time, they clambered to the top of the rock pile, then, even more cautiously, began to edge down the other side.

As they neared the ground, a sound met their ears — a low droning, so faint that at first Lief thought he was imagining it. And the next moment, without warning, he was below the cloud.

Slowly he turned away from the rocks to look at what was beyond. The breath caught in his throat. Sweat broke out on his forehead.

They had arrived at the Shifting Sands.

13 - The Shifting Sands

Sand. Nothing at all but deep, dry sand. As far as the eye could see, high red dunes rolled away under a low, brooding ceiling of murky yellow cloud. There was no sign of any living thing, but the low droning sound filled the place, as though the very air was alive.

Lief slithered down the last few rocks and his feet sank into the grainy softness beneath. A feeling of dread had settled over him — a feeling as strong and real as any taste or smell.

I have been here before.

This was the place he had seen in the vision of the future the opal had given him on the Plain of the Rats. The terror that had haunted his dreams was about to become reality. When? In an hour? A day? A week?

Through his fear, he heard Jasmine speaking. "It

97

is impossible," she was saying, as she jumped down beside him. "If the gem is hidden here, we will never find it!"

"The Belt will grow warm when the gem is near," Barda reminded her. He, too, was plainly sobered by the size of the task ahead, but refused to admit it. "We will mark the sand into sections and search it, square by square."

"That could take months!" Jasmine exclaimed. "Months — or even years!"

"No." Lief had spoken quietly, but they both turned to him. He struggled to keep his voice steady. "This gem is like the others. It has a terrible Guardian," he said, staring out at the still and secret dunes. "And the Guardian is already aware of us. I feel it."

Or is it the Belt that feels it? he thought, as he moved out into the sand, like someone in a dream. Is it the Belt that feels the danger?

But he dared not put his hands on the Belt of Deltora. He knew that if he touched the opal — if he saw the future again — he would turn and run.

He closed his eyes to shut out the sight of the barren land, the glowering sky. But beneath his lids he still saw red sand. And the hungry, jealous will that was drawing him to itself, as it drew everything, everything in this place to itself, was stronger than ever.

He began climbing the first dune. His feet sank

deeply into the rippled sand, making every step an effort. He struggled on.

"Lief!" he heard Jasmine cry. Her voice penetrated his dream, and he opened his eyes. But he did not stop.

"We have only to move on," he called, without looking back. "The Guardian is very near. We will not have to search for it. It will find us."

✳

In a very short time they were surrounded by high dunes and had lost sight of the rocks. But their trail showed clearly behind them, so they were not afraid of becoming lost.

They had discovered that the dunes were not as empty of life as they had supposed. Red flies crawled from the sand as they passed and flew up to settle on their hands, faces, arms, and necks, biting and stinging. Scarlet lizards with long blue tongues wriggled out of unseen holes and preyed in turn upon the flies.

"But what eats the lizards?" asked Jasmine, and drew her dagger.

Shortly after that they passed a strange object lying on the sand. It was round, leathery, flat, and wrinkled — like an empty bag, or a gigantic, flattened grape that had been split along one side.

"Is it some sort of seed pod?" wondered Barda, looking at it.

"Like no seed pod *I* have ever seen," Jasmine

muttered. Filli chattered nervously into her ear and Kree, riding on her shoulder, made a worried, clucking sound.

Lief's scalp was prickling. He was haunted by the feeling that they were being watched. Yet nothing moved but the flies and the lizards. There was no sound but the low, faint droning, which he had decided must be wind moaning around the dunes, though he could feel no breeze and the sand was still.

They had reached the bottom of one dune, and had just begun to climb another, when Jasmine, who was now in the lead, stiffened and held up her hand.

Barda and Lief stopped. At first they could hear nothing. And then, floating on the still air, there was a voice, growing louder by the moment.

"Carn 2! Never mind the flies. Keep moving!"

Lief looked frantically behind him. Their trail showed clearly in the sand. Their footprints were like arrows, pointing to their position. There was nowhere to hide. No escape.

The droning sound seemed to become a little louder, as though, Lief thought, the wind was excited by their fear. And just at that moment he remembered a trick he used to play back in Del. A trick that had fooled Grey Guards before, and, perhaps, could fool them again.

Gesturing to Barda and Jasmine to follow his

lead, he began to step backwards, carefully fitting his feet into his own footprints. When he had reached the bottom of the dune, he leaped to one side to lie motionless in its faint shadow.

His companions copied his every movement. When they were all huddled together, Lief covered them with his cloak, which blended quickly with the sand.

They waited, still as stones.

The Guards appeared, struggling in their heavy boots. They ran down the side of their dune, and began following the tracks up the next.

Then they stopped, puzzled. For, halfway up the dune, the tracks appeared to stop dead.

"They have been taken!" growled Carn 2. "As I told you they would be, Carn 8. I told you it was needless to follow them into the Shifting Sands. We are putting ourselves in danger for — "

"Be silent!" snapped his companion. "Do you not understand, you fool? We have disgraced the Carn pod. We let a Champion and two finalists escape. Our lives are worth nothing — less than nothing — unless we get them back. They may not have been taken. They could have buried themselves in the sand. Dig! Dig!"

He began to burrow into the sand with both hands. Grumbling, Carn 2 crouched to join him.

Then, suddenly, the dune seemed to erupt beneath them and, with shocking speed, a huge, hideous creature sprang from the collapsing sand and seized them, lifting them off their feet.

The Guards shrieked in terror. Paralyzed with shock, hardly able to believe their eyes, Lief, Barda, and Jasmine lay rigid beneath the concealing cloak. The monster had been perfectly hidden in the dune. Waiting. One more step, and they, instead of their enemies, would have been its prey.

Lief stared in fascinated horror. The creature was eight-legged, with a tiny head that seemed all mirrored eyes. Dozens of leathery bags, like the one they had seen lying on the ground, hung from its body. Sand still poured from its joints and crevices. It regarded its captives without curiosity as they struggled and swung in its terrifying grip. Then it opened its mouth, leaned forward . . . and abruptly, mercifully, the screaming and the struggling stopped.

It had all happened in seconds. Sickened by what they had seen, Lief, Barda, and Jasmine remained huddled under the cloak, not daring to move.

Delicately, using its pincers, the monster picked the clothes from the dead bodies of its prey, like a bird shelling snails. The companions watched as clothes, boots, money bags, Jasmine's medallion, metal canisters of blisters, slings, clubs, and water bottles thudded onto the sand. Then the creature sat back on its spiny haunches and began to eat, taking its time. Lizards and flies crawled out of the sand in the thousands to feast on the scraps that fell from its mouth.

Lief buried his face in his arms. He had no love for Grey Guards. But he could not watch this.

※

The lowering yellow cloud blotted out the sun so completely that Lief lost all sense of time. For what seemed like hours he, Barda, and Jasmine lay motionless while the creature ate its fill and slowly the bags hanging from its body swelled till they looked like gigantic grapes hanging from a stalk.

"They are stomachs!" breathed Barda in disgust. Lief shuddered. And even Jasmine, familiar with so many weird creatures in the Forests of Silence, wrinkled her nose with distaste.

At last, the flies and lizards scattered and the beast stood upright. One of the swollen stomachs, bigger than all the rest, tore away from its body and rolled to rest in the sand, leaving only a ragged stump behind. Seemingly unconcerned, the creature crawled forward and settled on top of it.

"What is it doing?" breathed Lief, unable to keep silent.

"I think it is piercing the stomach and laying an egg inside," Jasmine whispered back. "That way, the hatchling will have food while it grows."

Barda turned his head away.

But the sand beast had already finished its egg-laying and was moving again. Sluggishly, it ambled through the ruined dune in which it had hidden and climbed the next, soon disappearing over the top. The companions waited a moment to be sure it would not return, then climbed stiffly to their feet.

Without hesitation, but still gripping her dagger, Jasmine hurried over to where lizards and flies still swarmed over the Guards' bones and the blood-stained tatters of their clothes. Beating away the scavengers, she began rapidly sorting through the rags, putting aside in a small pile things that would be of use: the Guards' slings and blisters, their clubs and water bottles, the money bags. After a moment she looked up, startled.

"The money bags burst as they fell," she called in a low voice. "Most of the coins spilled out. But they are not here any longer. They are gone! And so has my medallion."

"That is impossible!" Barda strode towards her and himself began searching. Lief followed more slowly. His attention had been caught by a flat patch of sand just beyond where his friends were crouching. What he saw there made his flesh creep.

"The creature was blocking our view for hours as it fed," Jasmine was insisting. "Something or someone crawled in unseen and took — "

"It cannot be!" Barda was growing impatient as he fruitlessly searched the tumbled sand.

"Look!" Lief's voice sounded choked, even to himself. He cleared his throat, and pointed.

The smooth patch of sand was covered with hundreds of strange, circular marks. Marks that had not been there before.

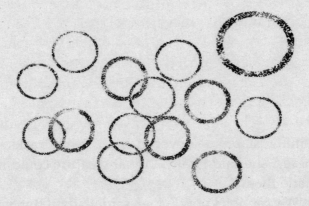

14 ~ Terror

Jasmine stared. "Never have I seen tracks like these," she said finally. "What creature could have made them?"

"We cannot know," Lief said flatly. "But whatever it is it is something that does not fear the sand beast, and something that likes gold. Perhaps it likes gems, too. Perhaps it is the Guardian."

"But surely the sand beast is the Guardian!" Barda exclaimed.

Jasmine shook her head. "I think it is just one of the creatures of the Sands," she said positively. "We have just seen it lay an egg. What is more, we passed an empty stomach skin on our way here. That hatchling had already emerged to fend for itself. There could be hundreds of sand beasts here. There could be thousands."

Barda cursed under his breath.

The low, droning sound drummed in Lief's ears. He stared at the circles on the sand. They seemed to mock him. He tried to look away, but his eyes kept being drawn back to them. He forced his gaze up to the sky — but there was no relief there. The unchanging roof of cloud seemed to press down on him, hemmed in as he was by faceless dunes. And all the time fear plucked at him like the flies which had returned in force, stinging, stinging . . .

Suddenly he could stand it no longer. With a muffled cry he leaped upon the tracks and kicked at them, destroying them, digging his heels deeply into the soft sand and scattering it everywhere.

"Lief! Stop!" he heard Barda call. But Lief was past listening. He shouted and fell to the ground, beating and tearing at it. Barda and Jasmine ran to him, trying to pull him to his feet. He fought them away.

There was a soft shifting sound and a low rumbling. Then the earth began to move. Lief heard Barda and Jasmine cry out. And just in time he grasped their hands as huge columns of sand began to thrust themselves upward all around them.

Jerked off their feet, the three tumbled together, rolling helplessly, blindly, as the sand roared and quaked beneath them. Lief could hear Jasmine screaming for Kree, and the bird's answering screech. He could hear his own voice, too, groaning in fear.

There is something here.

He knew it. He could see nothing, for his eyes

were tightly closed against the stinging sand, but he could feel a terrible, rage-filled presence all around him.

And he knew what it was. It was the thing that had been drawing him on. The thing that was hungry for what it sensed he could give it.

It wants the Belt . . . It will not rest until it has . . .

Then, suddenly, he felt the power withdraw. And immediately, as quickly as it had begun, the storm ceased and the ground quieted.

He lay still, dizzy and panting, as the last of the flying sand fell around him like rain.

With a rush of wings, Kree landed on Jasmine's arm. He was unharmed, though powdered all over with red dust. He began ruffling and preening his feathers, trying to clean himself. Filli chattered excitedly inside Jasmine's jacket. She murmured to him, calming him.

Lief brushed at his face with trembling hands.

"An earthquake," mumbled Barda. "So — that is why this place is called the Shifting Sands. We should have realized . . ."

"It was not an ordinary earthquake," snapped Jasmine. "It cannot simply be chance that Lief was kicking those marks away when it began. Lief, why did you do that? What is wrong with you? Are you ill?"

Lief could not answer. He was staring blankly around him.

Everything had changed. Dunes had collapsed and formed again in different places, and great valleys had opened where hills had been before. All tracks and signs that had previously marred the sands were gone. The ruined dune, the place where the Guards had died — both had disappeared.

He, Barda, and Jasmine may as well have been dropped from the sky into a part of the Sands they had never seen before. Only the low, droning sound was the same.

"Lief will not speak to me!" he heard Jasmine say to Barda in a frightened voice. She sounded very far away.

The sun was still blanketed by the clouds above. Lief could not tell which way was east and which way west. And he had been spun and tumbled so many times that he had no idea from which direction he had come.

So this is the beginning, he thought.

His glazed eyes fell on a mark in the sand, quite close to where he was lying. His throat seemed to close as he stared at it, and understood its meaning.

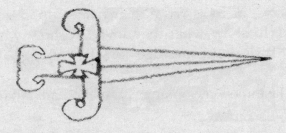

Lief felt Barda take him by the shoulder and shake him. He licked his lips and forced himself to speak. "Do not worry. I am all right," he said huskily.

"You do not seem all right," Barda growled. "You are acting as though you have lost your wits!"

"It is Jasmine who has lost something," murmured Lief. "She has lost her dagger — the dagger with the carved crystal set in the hilt."

"Oh, did you find it?" Jasmine exclaimed. "I am so glad. I dropped it just before the sandstorm ended. It was my father's. I thought it was gone for good!"

"So it is, I fear." Lief pointed to the drawing on the sand.

Jasmine and Barda gaped, speechless.

"The thing whose anger caused the storm accepted the dagger as tribute and left us in peace while it took it away," Lief murmured.

"The circles in the sand! They were not tracks, but pictures of the gold coins, and the medal!" Barda gritted his teeth. "What sort of creature is this? Why does it leave marks to show what it has taken?"

Lief shrugged. "Why do sculptors carve figures of stone, or shop owners list their wares upon their windows, or fools write their names upon trees and walls? To show what they love. To show what they own. To leave a message for all who pass by that way."

Jasmine was looking wary. "You are talking very

strangely, Lief," she said. "I do not like it. You speak as if you know this thing."

Lief shook his head. "It is beyond knowing," he said.

The verse they had seen carved on the stone at the crossroads kept running through his mind.

Death swarms within its rocky wall
Where all are one, one will rules all.
Be now the dead, the living strive
With mindless will to . . . survive.

He knew that he did not have the last lines quite right. But two words he was quite sure about.

Mindless will.

A thing of mindless will ruled the Shifting Sands and all that was precious in that fearsome place it gathered to itself. The terrifying creatures who shared its domain could have the flesh of their victims. The Guardian wanted only the treasure the victims carried.

For the first time since entering the Sands, Lief touched the Belt under his shirt, checking that the fastening was secure. As he did, his fingers brushed the topaz, and suddenly his mind cleared.

It was as though a dusty veil had been ripped from a window, allowing light and air to enter. But somehow he knew that the flash would not last long. There was another power at work here, and it was ancient and terrible.

He whirled around to Barda. "We must move on," he said urgently. "Light is fading, and the place we seek is far from here, for the Belt is not yet warm. But I want you to fasten us together so that we cannot be separated. I must be in the middle, tied very tightly."

Grimly, Barda did as he asked, using the rope they had bought from Mother Brightly. It was light, but very strong. Lief tested it, and nodded. "Do not release me, whatever I say," he muttered.

His companions nodded, asking no questions.

They drank a little water. Then they set off, weapons drawn, linked together by their lifeline, as darkness slowly fell.

※

The night brought no moon, no stars. The cloud hung above them black, black, and it was very cold. They had lit a torch, but the light it gave was small, and they jumped at every shadow. For a long time Barda and Jasmine had wanted to stop, but always Lief had urged them on.

At last, however, they refused to listen to him any longer.

"We cannot go on like this, Lief," Barda said firmly. "We must eat, and rest."

Lief stood shaking his head, swaying on his feet. All he wanted was to lie down, yet somehow he knew that if he slept he would be in danger.

But already Jasmine had untied her end of the

rope, dropped to her knees, and begun fumbling in her pack. In moments she had scraped a shallow hole in the sand and thrown the Guards' clubs into it.

"Never have these been put to better use," she said, laying the torch on top of the smooth, hard wood and adding some of Mother Brightly's fire chips for good measure. "Soon we will have a fine, cheering blaze."

She beckoned impatiently and Lief, unable to resist any longer, flopped down beside her. Barda, too, came to the fire. Seeing that Lief lay still, he groaned with relief, untied the binding cord from his own waist and stretched out.

The fire rose, crackling. The heavy sticks began to glow. The heat grew and spread.

Barda held out his hands. "Ah, wonderful!" he sighed with satisfaction.

And that was the last Lief heard. For the next moment, there was a great roar, the sand heaved, and the world about him seemed to explode.

15 - The Center

L
ief was alone, among rippling dunes that had no ending. He knew that somehow the night had passed. Light was filtering through the thick, yellow cloud. The sand beneath his feet was warm.

It was day. His terrible vision had come to pass, as he had always known it would.

He remembered the sand rising beneath him in darkness and tossing him into the air. He remembered the sound of Jasmine's and Barda's voices shouting his name. He remembered the burning coals of the fire spraying through the night, dying as they flew.

But that was all. Now there were only his own tracks trailing off into the distance over smooth, sandy wastes. Now there were only the dragging, useless tails of the rope still tied around his waist. Now there was only the droning sound, louder now, filling his ears, filling his mind.

He was clutching something in his hand. He looked down, and willed his fingers to open.

It was the painted wooden bird that Jasmine had put in her pocket in Rithmere. He must have found it, picked it up, after . . .

Numbly, he slipped the little object into the top pocket of his shirt. His legs were aching. His throat was parched — dry as the sand itself. His eyes were prickling. He could hardly see. He knew he must have walked for many hours, but he had no memory of it.

The Center.

He was being drawn towards the Center. That much he knew. His strength was almost gone. He knew that, too. But he could not stop, for if he stopped he would sleep. And if he slept, death would come. That he knew most of all.

He staggered on, reached the foot of another dune, took a step to begin climbing. Without warning his legs gave way underneath him and he fell. The sand cushioned him, soft as a feather bed. He rolled onto his back, but could move no farther.

Sleep.

His eyes closed . . .

In Del, friends are laughing, splashing in the choked and overflowing gutters, picking up gold coins. He wants to go to them. But his mother and father are calling . . . And now he sees that the gutters are choked not with garbage but with buzzing red bees. The gutters are overflowing with Queen Bee Cider that is pouring from broken barrels lying in the street, running to waste. The bees rise up in an angry cloud. His friends are being stung, and Grey Guards are watching, laughing . . . His friends are dying, calling to him, but he is so tired, so tired. His eyes keep closing as he staggers into the humming red cloud. His arms and legs are heavy, weighed down. Behind him his mother says, "Softly, softly, boy!" and he turns to her. But her face has turned into the face of Queen Bee. Bees cover her back and arms and swarm in her hair. She is frowning, screeching harshly at him, shaking her fist. "Smoke, not fire! Smoke, not fire . . ."

Lief's eyes flew open. The screeching went on. Something was circling high above him, a blurry black shape against a dull yellow sky.

Ak-Baba! Run! Hide!

Then he blinked, and saw that the circling shape was Kree — Kree, soaring lower, calling to him. He tried to sit up and found that he had settled so deeply into the sand that he had to wrench himself free. Sand had already covered the whole lower half of his body, his hands, his arms, his neck . . .

He scrambled, panting and trembling, to his feet. How long had he been asleep? What would have happened if Kree had not woken him? Would he have slipped deeper and deeper into the sand until at last it covered him? Would he have woken even then?

The dream was still vivid in his mind. And suddenly he understood what it meant. The words of the verse rushed back to him. "Not 'be now,' but 'below,' " he whispered. "Not 'survive,' but . . ."

"Lief!" Barda and Jasmine had appeared at the top of the next dune. Shouting, they began to slide down towards him. Lief felt tears spring into his eyes at the sight of them, and realized that he had thought they were dead. He began staggering forward to meet them.

Jasmine screamed, piercingly. She was pointing behind him.

He turned, and saw what had emerged from the dune at his back. It was another sand beast, even bigger than the first. Sand still poured from the joints of its legs. It had been stalking him, but as he met its mirrored eyes it froze. In moments, he knew, it would spring.

Backing away, holding its gaze, he felt for his sword, then, with horror, felt himself falling clumsily, entangled in the trailing ropes that had tripped him. The next moment he was struggling in the sand, his sword trapped beneath him. Wildly he scrambled to his knees, hearing Jasmine and Barda shouting, knowing it was too late, feeling as though he was caught in a nightmare. The monster lurched forward . . .

Then it jerked, with a grating cry, as a blister exploded on its body. It staggered, lunged again, then toppled sideways as another blister found its mark. Its spiny legs kicked, and it began to spin, digging great trenches in the sand.

One ankle still caught in the rope, Lief crawled away, sobbing and gasping with relief. Jasmine came panting up to him, hauling him to his feet, freeing him from the rope. Barda was right behind her, a sling still in his hand and another blister at the ready.

Lief began to choke out his thanks, but Barda waved him away. "If I have saved your life, Lief, it is not the first time, nor will it be the last, I fear," he growled. "It is my fate, it seems, to be your nurse-maid."

Shocked and deeply hurt, Lief took refuge in sullenness, and turned away.

Barda took him by the shoulder and spun him around. "Do not turn away from me!" he shouted. "What are you playing at? Why did you run away alone? Why did you not try to find us after the quake?"

He was shaking with anger. And slowly Lief realized that it was the anger born of shock, fear, and worry. It was the anger he had sometimes seen in his parents' faces, when he came home long after curfew. When he took risks.

"Barda, I could not — " he began.

"There is no time for this now," snapped Jasmine, her eyes on the monstrous creature thrashing in the dune. "Argue another time. We must get away from here, and quickly. The beast is not dead. It may yet recover and come after us again."

"Do not worry," said Lief quietly. "Where we are going, it will not follow."

✳

They walked for many hours, but spoke little. It was as if Lief was listening to something that neither Barda nor Jasmine could hear, and they themselves grew more and more silent the closer they came to the Center.

They saw it long before they reached it — a lone peak rising high from a flattened circle and ringed by rounded dunes. It shimmered against the yellow sky, alien and mysterious in the fading light. A mighty cone with darkness at its tip.

"A volcano," hissed Barda.

Lief shook his head. "You will see," he said.

Filli crept, whimpering, under the shelter of Jasmine's collar. She whispered comfortingly to him, but her green eyes were dark with dread.

The droning noise grew louder as they approached their goal. By the time they had reached its base and slowly begun to labor upwards, the air was vibrating with sound.

And finally they had reached the top, and were looking down into the peak's hollow core. A whirlpool of red sand roared far below, flying in the darkness as though driven by a mighty wind.

But there was no wind. And the sound was like the humming of bees in their countless millions.

The Belt burned around Lief's waist.

"What is this?" Barda was breathing hard, staring down, his big, blunt hands gripping his sword.

Softly Lief repeated the rhyme carved on the stone. And this time, the last lines were complete.

"Death swarms within its rocky wall
Where all are one, one will rules all.
Below the dead, the living strive
With mindless will to serve the Hive."

"The Hive . . ." Jasmine repeated slowly.

"The Sand is the Guardian," said Lief.

Barda shook his head. "But — it cannot be," he breathed. "The sand is not alive! We have walked upon it, seen creatures — "

"The creatures we have seen are crawling on a much larger host," said Lief, his voice very low. "The dunes we have been treading are only a covering, made up of the long dead. The living work below. Serving the Hive. It is they who collect the treasures that fall. It is they who make the marks on the surface. They who cause the storms."

"The gem — "

"The gem, dropped anywhere on the Sands, would at last be drawn to the Center," Lief murmured. "That is why we are here."

He tore his eyes away from the whirlpool within

the core and turned to Jasmine. "We need smoke," he said. "Smoke, not fire."

Without a word she knelt and began pulling things from her pack. Her hands, Lief saw, were trembling.

His own hands were not very steady as he gave his sword to Barda and took the rope in exchange. But as he knotted the rope around his chest, he was half-smiling, and his voice shook only a little.

"I fear you must be my nursemaid again, Barda," he said. "Again I need your help and your strength — and your rope as well. But this time, I beg you, do not let me go."

16 - The Cone

Lief crawled over the lip of the pit and stepped into empty space. He dangled, swinging gently to and fro, looking up at Barda's and Jasmine's worried faces and their hands, the knuckles white, gripping the rope.

"Slowly," he mouthed. He saw them nod, and their hands move. Then, gently, he began to sink through the core of the cone.

Lief's cloak was bound tightly around him and its hood was drawn closely around his head and face, covering all but his eyes. I must look like a big grub in a cocoon, he thought. But no grub would be so foolish as to invade a hive. If it did . . .

Shuddering, he turned his mind to other things.

Smoke from the dampened torch, well padded with wet rags, billowed around him. He was not certain it would help, but certainly no other weapon would be useful here. Besides, ever since his dream, Queen Bee's words had kept coming back to him, and surely that was for a reason.

My guards do not like sudden movements, and are easily angered. Why, even I must use smoke to calm them when I take their honey from the Hive . . .

He could remember the words so clearly. Strangely, here, at the droning, swirling hub of the Sands, his mind had cleared and sharpened. Perhaps the Hive was no longer calling him, because it had no need. He was where it had wanted him to be all along.

He looked up. His friends' faces were tiny now. He was hardly able to see them against the glare of the sky. And below, the seething mass that was the Hive was whirling, rising to meet him.

He braced himself, closed his eyes. Then he felt it, like a hot, rough wind, a stinging whirlwind, sucking him in. It spun savagely about him, whipping him, pressing in on him, with a sound like thunder.

It was too strong. Too strong!

He could not see. He could not breathe. Spun in a raging torrent of sound, he did not know which way was up, which down. He knew only one thing:

The Hive cared nothing for him. To the Hive he was not food, or a captive prize, or even a hated enemy to be defeated. To the Hive he was nothing but the carrier of the thing it desired. The Hive would suffocate him. It would rub the clothes from his flesh and the flesh from his bones. Then it would have what it wanted. What it had wanted from the beginning.

The Belt of Deltora.

Panic gripped Lief by the throat. He began to struggle, to scream —

Softly, boy, softly. Gently, gently!

The crabbed old voice was as clear in his mind as if it had spoken right beside his ear. It was like cold water splashed in his face.

The screams died in his throat. He opened his eyes. He forced himself to be still, to stop gasping for air, to breathe evenly.

He opened his eyes a fraction. Through the narrow slits he saw that the smoke pouring from the torch had at last begun mingling with the whirling red.

And the whirlwind was quieting. The Hive was slowing, and thinning. It was retreating to the darkness at the sides of the cone. And the thing that its fury had previously hidden was at last revealed — a glistening pyramid rising through the cone's center.

Slowly, carefully, Lief reached up and tugged the rope once. His downward progress stopped with a slight jolt as, far above, Jasmine and Barda received the signal.

For a moment he simply swung in space, staring, fascinated, through the drifting smoke, at the astounding thing the living Sand had built, tended, and guarded for years without number.

It was a towering pyramid of cells made of gold, glass, gems, and bleached, white bones.

Lief told himself that he had expected this — or something like it. But the reality was beyond anything he could have imagined.

Anything that would not decay, or would decay so slowly that it would have to be replaced only after centuries, had been gathered and used for the building. Skulls and bones of every shape and size were packed side by side with glass bottles and jars, coins, crystals and gems, gold chains, rings and bracelets, and yet more bones. The individual parts, small and large, had been fitted together with such care that the tower glittered like an enormous jewel.

It was an awesome sight. And unbelievably horrible.

It was a pyramid of death. How many human beings had been stripped of life for its sake? And what was stored inside those secret cells? The Hive's young, no doubt. Eggs, then tiny squirming things, packed in the thousands, nursed and cared for, fed on a disgusting brew of decayed red flies, dead lizards, and whatever else slipped beneath the sand. Till they grew into — what? Not insects of any kind he had ever known. Not insects at all, perhaps. Some other form of life he could not even imagine. Some tiny unit that would become part of the ancient thing that had lived on while all around it changed. The Hive.

Shaken with disgust, Lief ached to kick and tear

at the tower, to see it fall and smash to pieces in the darkness below. In that darkness, no doubt, the giant Hive Queen lurked. He almost felt he could see her bloated shape, rippling in the depths, laying eggs, eggs without number.

But he knew that if he attacked the pyramid the Hive would be upon him. The smoke would not hold it back.

And the Belt was throbbing and burning. Somewhere in this gleaming tower lay the gem he was seeking. Was it the diamond? The amethyst? The emerald? He could see clear, purple, and green stones among those that sparkled in the pyramid. But which was the precious One?

He pulled his cloak and shirt aside to reveal the Belt, and looked down at it, peering through wreaths of smoke. He could hardly see the topaz and the ruby. But the opal shone, dancing with sparkling lights so that it seemed alive.

What did that mean? He struggled to see in his mind the words about the powers of the opal in *The Belt of Deltora.*

✝ **The opal, symbol of hope, shines with all the colors of the rainbow. It has the power to give glimpses of the future, and to aid those with weak sight. The opal . . .**

What came next? Lief screwed his eyes tightly closed to help him to think, but after a moment he opened them again, shaking his head desperately. He could not remember the end.

He looked up to the top of the pyramid. He knew that the gem was most likely to be there. It had been dropped into the Shifting Sands just before King Endon was overthrown. That was only a little over sixteen years ago, and the pyramid had been growing for many ages.

The first thing he saw was Jasmine's dagger, fitted point downwards into the very tip of the tower. It had been the last thing taken, so was at the top. One day the metal would rust away. But the crystal cross would survive, and other finds would take the place of the metal parts.

Below the dagger, neatly arranged, were many gold coins, and the Champion medal from the Rithmere Games. They were locked in place with a mass of shining white bones.

Lief shuddered. Not a scrap of flesh still clung to the bones, but he knew that they were all that remained of Carn 2 and Carn 8, the Grey Guards. The Hive worked quickly.

He realized that the pyramid seemed clearer than it had before. For a moment he wondered why that was. Then he saw that the torch was smoking less. It was starting to die.

His stomach lurched. For how much longer would the Hive stay droning at the sides of the cone? As the smoke thinned . . .

He looked below the bones and saw some small glass pots, some bracelets, two rocks, and what looked like the jawbone of a horse. And below that —

His heart seemed to miss a beat. There, pinpoints of light piercing its smooth, dark blue surface, was a stone like a starry night sky.

The forgotten words from *The Belt of Deltora* flashed at last into his mind.

. . . The opal has a special relationship with the lapis lazuli, the heavenly stone, a powerful talisman.

The lapis lazuli! There it lay, carefully wedged into place, supporting the roof of an as yet empty cell. The fourth gem of the Belt of Deltora.

He reached for it, then abruptly drew back his hand. If he pulled the stone from its place, the things resting upon it would surely topple and fall. Then the Hive would attack. He would be dead before he could carry his prize to the surface, and the lapis lazuli, and the Belt itself, would be lost.

His only hope was to replace the gem with something else. Something of about the same size. Frantically, he felt in his pockets, though he knew he had nothing — nothing . . .

Then his fingers touched something in the top pocket of his shirt. Something small, hard, and oddly shaped. He pulled it out.

It was Jasmine's little wooden bird. And it was just the right size.

The Hive droned with growing suspicion. It was waking, becoming active, as the smoke began to disappear. Holding his breath, Lief reached again for the lapis lazuli. But this time he grasped in his other hand the little wooden bird.

He eased the lapis lazuli from its place. It warmed in his fingers, and moved easily, more easily than he expected, as though it wanted to be free.

The opal is calling it, he thought, feeling the answering warmth at his waist. He felt the lapis lazuli slip into his hand, and quickly pushed the little wooden bird into its place.

Not quickly enough. The top of the tower trembled. The droning from the walls of the cone became louder, more alert. The red cloud swayed inward. Its outside edge just touched the bare skin of Lief's chest, searing, burning. He smothered a scream of anguish.

Quietly, quietly . . .

Sweat dripping into his eyes, trying to screen out the pain, Lief lifted a hand and tugged at the rope. Once, twice . . . Beside him, the pyramid swayed. If it should fall. If anything should fall . . .

The dagger toppled from its place, turning in the air. Lief snatched at it one-handed, just managing to catch it by its tip as he rose beside it, the dying torch tucked under one arm.

129

With agonizing slowness, he was drawn to the surface. Below him, the droning sound was rumbling, rising, as the Hive closed in, circling the pyramid once more. The Hive did not yet know it had been robbed. It was still sleepy and distracted because smoke still drifted in the air. The smoke was faint now, so faint . . .

But it was still working its magic as Lief crawled into the fresh air above.

And as he stood up and turned joyously to Barda and Jasmine, as he opened his hand to show them the heavenly stone, the clouds that had covered the sky flew apart like torn rags. The stars and the moon beamed down again upon the dark earth like a blessing, and the lapis lazuli sparkled back at them like a tiny mirror.

It slipped into the Belt and glowed there, alive under the moon.

Lief turned to Jasmine. "I had to leave your little bird behind. But I brought you this in exchange," he said softly, and gave her the dagger. Wordlessly she took it, slipped it inside her jacket, and held it close.

Lief swayed and Barda gripped his arm. "The lapis lazuli is a talisman, Barda," Lief whispered. "We will be safe now. But let us leave this place."

❊

Lief said little else as the companions walked slowly down the smooth red of the peak. At the bottom he let Jasmine smooth healing balm over the raw patches on his chest. It eased the pain a little. It made the long journey back to the edge of the Sands bearable.

They had the stars to guide them now. They had the lapis lazuli to offer protection against the dangers of the night. But it was not until they had reached the rocks that edged the Sands, and had climbed out onto solid land, that Lief was able to speak of what he had seen.

"Thank the heavens that you and the Belt are safe," murmured Barda when he had finished.

"And now," said Jasmine more cheerfully, "we have the fourth stone. Only three more to go. And surely they will be easy, compared to this."

Lief was silent. It was some moments before his friends realized that he was asleep.

"They *will* be easy, compared to this," Jasmine insisted, turning to Barda.

Barda was looking down at Lief's exhausted, sleeping face. He was thinking how much older the boy looked. He was thinking of all they had been through. What might yet be to come.

Jasmine would not be ignored. She tugged at his sleeve. "Barda! Do you not agree?" she demanded.

Barda was not wearing the Belt. The opal could not give him glimpses of the future. But a shadow crossed his face and his smile was grim as he answered.

"We shall see, Jasmine," he said. "We shall see."